A GEEKS AND THINGS COZY MYSTERY

Pains and Penalties

S.E. BIGLOW

❄ Created with Vellum

1

Kalina Greystone stood behind the counter bent over a tablet double checking inventory when her nephew, AJ, appeared in the doorway to what used to be the stockroom. He toted a box of comics in his arms. She was converting it into a gaming space and mini theater. "This was all that was left, Aunt K."

Setting the tablet aside, she gave him a smile. "I'll take those."

He handed the box over and she settled it below the counter on the top shelf. It contained all of the unclaimed new arrivals for her customers. It still amazed her that she could call them *her* customers. Coming home to run the family's comic store hadn't been in her five-year plan after graduating business school, but life had a way of intervening when it seemed most inconvenient and guiding her to where she was needed most. AJ peered at the tablet and pointed to the paper file sitting next to it. "What are you doing?"

"Going digital. Your grandpa kept paper ledgers of everyone's orders and what we had in stock. I just finished transferring everything to the tablet so we can move some of the old files to your mom's basement." She motioned to the counter space that had until three months ago housed a clumsy, old-fashioned cash register. "And thanks to Square, we can do all of our business on the tablet, too. Send e-receipts, the whole thing."

"Damn, you really are going high tech. Guess that fancy MBA really paid off."

"Don't swear." She nudged his shoulder. "We

still have a cash drawer, obviously, but it will be easier to reconcile at the end of the day."

AJ stepped behind the counter and pulled her into an unexpected hug. She returned the gesture if a little awkwardly. "What was that for?"

He shrugged one shoulder and didn't meet her gaze. "Nothing. Just missed you is all. Mom's glad you're back. Even if she doesn't say it."

"I missed you guys, too." Kalina often wondered if the relatively small age difference—18 years—between her and AJ made him see her as more of a friend than an authority figure. Still, she couldn't deny she liked hanging out with him. "And I know she's happy she didn't have to take over the business. Now go make sure we have everything ready for the booth at the fair."

Before they could continue their conversation, the front door opened and the tiny bell tinkled to announce the customer's entrance. AJ disappeared back through the game room and Kalina turned to greet the first patron of the day. Usually Saturdays were busy, especially in the morning, but today was the exception. Everyone was heading down to the waterfront for the annual Solstice Fair to kick off the start of summer. People from neighboring towns came out to the little town of Ellesworth, Massachusetts to enjoy arguably the best homemade baked goods on the southern coast of the state and generally indulge in silly carnival games. A familiar face greeted her and warmth crept up her neck. Christian Harper.

"Hi." Her mouth went dry at the sight of him. They hadn't really spoken in the last fifteen years. Not since they'd ended their three-year relationship in high school. But he looked just the same with his bright blue eyes—the kind a girl could get lost in without trying—and slightly messy brown hair.

"Hey, Kal. How are you?"

Kalina coughed a time or two to find her voice. "Good. Busy... Well, I mean not at this particular moment with the fair today but..."

She rambled when she was nervous. Taking a breath, she collected herself. "Can I help you with something, Officer?" Last she'd heard he had joined the police department out of college. Just because they hadn't spoken didn't mean she hadn't had ways of keeping up-to-date with his life. She'd also heard he was still single.

Chris smiled, his eyes crinkling around the corners. "Actually, it's Detective now." He tapped the top of his detective's shield. "And I was looking for some T-shirts for my nephews. They're big into superheroes these days."

"Nephews?" Kalina buried her face in her hands. How had she forgotten? "Of course. How old are they now?"

"Jackson is eight and Benji is ten."

She looked around the shop. The wall that normally housed the T-shirt selection was bare. "Well, we have some but we are taking them down to the fair. We have a booth."

"Well, if you don't mind the company, I'll go down with you. We can catch up."

"Sure. Let me just let AJ know he can head down and start setting up."

She was about to text him when AJ stuck his head in through the front door. "We're all set. Everything's in the car."

Kalina retrieved the locked cash box her father had kept for the fair from its spot on the back shelf. Holding it up, she gave it a shake. "You forgot this."

"I thought you said we were going digital?"

"Some things are tradition. Besides, you know all the proceeds from today go to the Wounded Warrior charity."

Her nephew rolled his eyes but grabbed the box and gestured for her to hand over the car keys. She arched a brow and nodded in Chris's direction. "I don't think so." She turned to Chris. "Want a ride?"

"Love one."

AJ led the small procession out of the shop. Kalina paused long enough to lock the front door—habits from her time living in the city— and climbed into the driver seat. Chris slid into the passenger and AJ settled in the back amidst the boxes of merchandise up for sale.

The trip down to the waterfront was brief and quiet. Apparently, 'catching up' didn't involve talking in front of a fifteen-year-old boy. Ten minutes later, Kalina's car was empty and the small booth with a "Geeks and Things" banner was laden with boxes. AJ wandered off in search of his friends, leaving the grown-ups to handle unpacking.

"I thought he was supposed to be helping you," Chris said as he laid out some new comics.

She waved dismissively in the direction he'd gone. "He'll be back. We're splitting our time so I figure he can get in on some rides before the lines get too long. What superheroes are the boys into?"

Chris scratched his chin. "Jack likes Hulk. And I'm pretty sure Benji mentioned something about Rocket Raccoon."

She rifled through a box of shirts. "So ... Detective, huh? Congrats."

"Thanks. I owe a lot to Captain Cahill. He trained me since I joined the force." That wasn't a name Kalina recognized, but there had been changes in leadership since she left to pursue her dreams of owning her own business.

"I bet." She nodded toward his badge. "You working today?" She found a couple of kids' smalls and held them up for his approval.

He gave her a thumbs up on both. "Sort of. But my shift doesn't start until later this afternoon." He smiled again and Kalina's legs went weak. "You know, Kal, I was honestly surprised to hear you'd come back to town."

She tugged at a few strands of loose, red curls. Could she admit to him she hadn't entirely wanted to? Would that make her sound like an awful daughter? "Well, Dad left the place to me in the will. I couldn't just leave it to wither away. He raised me on comics. It's in my blood."

"I'm sorry about your dad's passing by the way."

Her chest tightened for a moment at the

thought of her father's death. "Thanks. We knew he had heart trouble so the last heart attack wasn't a huge surprise. But it means a lot that you care."

More familiar faces passed by. Some waved or nodded in their direction. Kalina waved back. Despite not having wanted to come home, a part of her was happy to be back. She missed being a part of such a small community. She stowed the cash box behind a pile of old video games and leaned forward on the edge of the table. "So, you aren't on duty for a while. You want to check out the judging for the pastries?"

"Absolutely. How much do I owe you for the shirts?"

Kalina started to say they were free but caught herself. "Five bucks each."

He handed over a twenty dollar bill but waved her off when she made a move to open the cash box. "Consider the rest a donation."

"Thanks."

AJ appeared from the crowd and ducked

into the booth. His cheeks were flushed and he wore a dopey grin. The wrist band on his left hand signaled he'd been on the roller coaster and likely the Ferris wheel already. Kalina thought she spotted a smudge on his cheek that bore a strong resemblance to lipstick but she kept silent

"We'll be back. We're just going to check out the baking contest," Kalina said and patted her nephew on the shoulder. The contest had always been a favorite for her, especially since her great aunt Agatha and her friends had a habit of winning.

The fairgrounds bustled with people stopping by vendors on both sides of the promenade, buying everything from handmade picture frames to tote bags with hand-painted waterscapes. The pastry judging tent sat at the far end of the promenade. They always did the judging early on to encourage people to buy the winning sweets. It was never that much of a real competition. Mrs. Margaret Grant always won for her blueberry and raspberry scones. It had been that way since Kalina was a little girl. Usually, Kalina'a great aunt Agatha also won for her European sponge cake with lemon drizzle. Her mouth watered at the thought of the cake. She'd been away for the last few summers and had missed getting to share a slice while they chatted. Kalina walked with purpose towards the judging tent until she felt a hand squeeze lightly on her wrist.

"Sorry," she said when she saw Chris slowing her down. "I guess I still have some city habits to break."

"It's okay. You just don't need to be in such a hurry. You know they announce the winners over the loudspeaker."

She smiled sheepishly and fell into step beside him. The sun peeked out from behind a thin layer of cloud cover, highlighting thin veins of gold in Chris's hair. For a moment she remembered them as two high school kids who thought they were in love. But that time was past. They weren't kids anymore, maybe friends but nothing more. Not after she was sure she'd broken his heart when she went away to school. "So, did you ever settle down?"

"Nope. Still a bachelor. I guess I just never found the right girl. What about you?"

She shook her head. "There was a guy in college but ... it didn't end well."

They reached the judging tent and found both great aunt Agatha and Mrs. Grant sitting behind their respective entries. Kalina bent down to place an order for Mrs. Grant's scones and noticed another set of scones down the table manned by Andrea Nevins. She'd been a couple years ahead of Kalina and Chris in school.

"Nice to see you finally made it home, Kali," great aunt Agatha said with a smile. She reached out to pat Kalina on the wrist.

"Me, too, Auntie Agatha." She grabbed the pen in front of the sponge cake and jotted down an order as well. Agatha arched a silver brow. "Well, this is new. You don't usually buy my cake."

Kalina smirked. "Well, maybe I felt a little

guilty about missing the last few years. And honestly, it looks even better than usual."

"You're sweet, my girl." She gestured over Kalina's shoulder. "I see you two found your way back to each other."

Great aunt Agatha had always been fond of Chris. She was the first person Kalina had confided in when they'd started dating in school. "He just came by the shop to buy some shirts for his nephews. That's all."

"I told you that you two had something special. But I'm just an old lady, what do I know." She feigned annoyance but Kalina could see the sparkle in her eyes.

"You were never much of a match maker, Aggie," Mrs. Grant chided from her spot down the table.

"Oh hush, you," Agatha replied, waving her friend's comment away.

Kalina looked around, hoping to spot the third member of Aunt Agatha's trio, Cynthia Ellicott. For as long as she could remember, the three women had been inseparable and they never missed the Solstice Fair. "Where's Ms. Ellicott?"

Aunt Agatha and Mrs. Grant shared a look that Kalina couldn't decipher. "She hasn't been in the best health," Mrs. Grant answered quickly.

"Oh, I'm sorry to hear that. Is there anything I can do?"

Aunt Agatha shook her head. "No, when she gets like this, it's best to just give her space. But, it's sweet of you to worry. You always had such a kind heart, Kali."

Kalina darted around the side of the table and wrapped her aunt in a firm hug. "I'll see you later."

"I'll save you a big slice of cake," she replied with a wink.

"Well, good luck to both of you," Kalina said and stepped back to allow other people to approach. At the far end of the table, a man in a police uniform stood beside someone Kalina didn't recognize. "Who is that?" She addressed Chris and pointed at the pair.

"That's Captain Dan Cahill and the woman is his fiancée, Leslie Mayfield. She teaches at the elementary school. Benji is in her class."

They moved down the table and Chris placed an order for Leslie's apple tarts. "Good luck."

Leslie tucked a piece of hair behind her ear, not so subtly flashing her engagement ring, and smiled big. She turned to Kalina and offered her non-bejeweled hand. "Hi, I don't think we've met."

"I'm Kalina Greystone." They shook hands briefly. "My father used to own Geeks and Things up on Main Street. I moved back to run the store after he died."

"Oh, right, of course."

Dan leaned in and kissed Leslie on the cheek. "I think they're about to start the judging."

Kalina and Chris moved back into the crowd while the judges sampled the various sweets, concurring in low whispers and making notes on their clipboards. The town took the contest very seriously. Tension rose amongst the crowd as they awaited the announcement. At the far end of the table great aunt Agatha sat with her hands folded in her lap. Mrs. Grant shot Andrea annoyed looks as the judges handed the winning votes to the announcer, Theodore Maxwell. He cleared his throat and held the microphone too close to his mouth.

"We have the results of the baking contest. Remember, you can put an order in at any time to purchase the winning pastries. All proceeds go to the Wounded Warrior charity."

The feedback on the speakers squealed and Kalina covered her ears along with many of the people watching. Theo held the mic further from his mouth and studied the first scrap of paper. "The winner for best fruit tart goes to Ms. Leslie Mayfield."

Cheers went up from the crowd and Leslie grinned and waved. Captain Cahill let out a loud whistle, making his fiancée blush. He darted up to the stage and placed a huge bouquet in her arms. Theo waved his hand for quiet and the crowd settled down. "Best sponge cake, of course, goes to Mrs. Agatha Davies." The crowd's response was a little more subdued as Agatha stood up and took a little bow. Kalina noted the older woman's cheeks were a bit flushed when they hadn't been a few moments earlier. But she assumed it was just due to the excitement of yet another blue ribbon for her mantle. Beside Agatha, Mrs. Grant already had her hands on the armrest, poised to push herself up to accept the blue ribbon for her scones.

"And finally, the winner for the best scones is..." Theo stopped and turned to the judges. They nodded in unison and he faced the growing throng, clearing his throat as he did so. "The winner is Ms. Andrea Nevins."

A hush fell over the crowd. Mrs. Grant jumped from her seat and marched toward the judges before Andrea could accept the ribbon. Chris stood beside Kalina, mouth agape as the older woman leaned in close enough to Theo's microphone that her tirade carried across the fairgrounds.

"This is unacceptable. My scones were far better than hers."

Andrea paled and dabbed her eyes before hurrying off the stage clutching the ribbon to her chest. A few members in the crowd patted her on the back and her older brother broke from the group to wrap an arm around her shoulders, leading her away.

"Mrs. Grant, please. This is just a friendly competition," Theo said, trying to yank the microphone out of her reach.

She wasn't having any of it. She waggled a finger at the judges, summoning them forward. "You three had better explain yourselves."

From behind her, great aunt Agatha shuffled forward and tried to tug Mrs. Grant away but had no luck. "Margie, come on now." Agatha's words fell of deaf ears.

"It's not that your scones weren't good, Mrs. Grant. It's just ... Andy's were better this year," one of the judges said.

People began to disperse, no longer interested in seeing Mrs. Grant lose her temper with the judges. Kalina nudged Chris in the ribs and nodded back towards the booth. "I should probably head back to make sure AJ is doing okay." She looked at her watch. "Besides, he's probably looking for an early lunch."

"No problem."

They walked side by side back down the promenade. Kalina made a mental note to stop by some of the booths near the end of the day to pick up some early Christmas presents for her sister and mother. The Geeks and Things booth came into view and she couldn't keep a smile from tugging at the corners of her lips. A small group of kids clamored around the table, picking up action figures and T-shirts. Money changed hands rapidly and AJ gave her a double thumbs up when he spotted her.

"Well, I'll leave you to hawking your wares," Chris said.

"Enjoy the rest of the fair." She waved and slid in behind the table next to her nephew.

He blew out a breath. "Thank God you're back. It's been super nuts. I'm starving."

Kalina chuckled. "Yes, yes. Go get food. Bring me back a fried dough. Extra cinnamon sugar."

He gave her a salute and raced out of the booth and toward the refreshment tent. Kalina settled into the metal chair behind the table and waited for people passing by to stop. She didn't have to wait long before Leslie appeared with her big smile plastered to her lips. She'd pinned the ribbon to her blouse. The bouquet was nowhere to be seen.

"Congrats again on your win," Kalina said.

"Thanks. I'm sorry I didn't recognize you before. I guess I'm not all that good with faces unless they are my students."

"No worries. I left town for a while after high school. Big city dreams. Earned my business degree and worked in Boston for a few years. But I guess my heart was always back here in town." Maybe if she told herself that enough time, it would make it sure. Kalina glanced around for Captain Cahill. "Where's your fiancé?"

"Oh, getting some drinks from the refreshment tent. We're going to celebrate. Did you want to buy some fruit tarts?"

"Sure. I'd love to."

Their conversation died instantly when a high-pitched shriek went up from the direction of the food. Another scream followed it. Leaving cash box and merchandise untended, Kalina took off at a sprint. Thoughts of AJ spurred her forward. She didn't bother to check to see if Leslie was following or not. Kalina arrived at the tent to find people bunched together in a semi-circle around one of the tables. Kalina shoved her way to the front. AJ bent over a motionless great aunt Agatha. She lay on the ground, one hand pressed to her stomach, the other gripped around her throat. She'd already started to lose color in her cheeks. AJ looked up, his facial features contorted into a mask of helpless terror, and he said, "I think she's dead."

2

Footsteps pounded on the hard-packed ground and Chris came into view. Kalina had no idea where he'd come from but he didn't look out of breath. On the other side of the table, Mrs. Grant pressed one hand to her chest, tears glistening in her eyes. She'd calmed down from her rant about the scones but now that same look of horror Kalina had seen in her nephew's eyes reflected in the old woman's.

"Dear Lord, this can't be happening."

It was barely audible above the crowd

yelling for help, but Kalina heard it. The statement seemed an odd reaction and it piqued her curiosity. Kalina bent down and gently tugged AJ to his feet and away from Agatha's prone form. Chris took up AJ's spot and studied her. "Who saw what happened?"

AJ raised his hand. His fingers trembled and he quickly closed them into a fist to keep from shaking. A few other people inched forward, mumbling that they had seen what happened. From across the tent Captain Cahill approached, cell phone in hand. He pressed it to his ear and, amid the rumbling of the crowd, Kalina heard him request an ambulance. Ellesworth wasn't big enough to have its own morgue. She'd no doubt be taken west to Salem. Chris stood up and waved people back. "Everyone, I need you to back up. Do not touch anything on this table." He turned to AJ. "I'm going to need to talk to you. Why don't you come with me?"

"I'm coming with him," Kalina said.

"Did you see anything?"

"No. But you can't talk to him alone. He's only fifteen." She didn't think Chris thought AJ had done anything bad, but she also knew her nephew needed support and she wasn't going to let him go through witnessing a close relative just drop dead.

Chris looked unhappy about the intrusion but didn't object further. They headed over to an empty table at the back of the tent while Captain Cahill ushered the rest of the crowd out of the food tent. He disappeared as well, only to be heard moments later over the loudspeaker.

"Ladies and gentlemen, I'm sorry to announce we will be shutting down early this year. Due to a medical emergency, we ask that all vendors please conclude your transactions and pack up."

This was not how Kalina had expected her first time running the booth in her own right would go. Turning her attention back to Chris and AJ, she reached over and squeezed her nephew's hand.

"Okay, AJ. Walk me through what you saw." Chris produced a notepad from his pocket. He came prepared for anything. His tone was gentle, supportive.

"I was in line for fried dough. Aunt K. wanted some, and auntie Agatha was sitting there having a cup of tea. She gave me a wave and I was going to stop by and see her before I headed back to the booth. Everything was fine and then she just started choking and bent over like she was going to throw up." He put his head in his hands. "I never saw anyone look like that."

Kalina took one of his hands in hers and gave it a firm squeeze. "It's okay. You did good."

He looked up at her through watery eyes. "But... I should have done something to help."

"Had you seen her before today? I know your family was close," Chris probed.

"Uh, maybe a week ago she came by for dinner with me and my parents."

"And how'd she seem then?"

"Fine. Why?"

"I'm just trying to get a sense of what might have made her start choking." Chris glanced at the table she'd bee sitting at. "You said she had tea. Was she eating anything?"

"No. Just the tea."

Chris leaned over. "Did you see anyone tamper with her tea?"

"N-no. I don't think so. God, was she murdered?" His teenage falsetto shot his voice up an octave.

Chris shook his head. "I don't know. But something happened to make her stop breathing." Chris tucked his notepad in his pocket. " I'd like you go down to the station and give a full statement."

"Does he have to do it right now? He's in shock," Kalina argued.

Chris's face softened. "No. Just make sure you get down there in the next day or so. If this turns out to be something more than accidental then we want to get people's recollections down as clearly as possible."

Kalina stared at him in confusion. He

couldn't honestly believe someone would want to hurt aunt Agatha. She'd probably just choked on the tea and couldn't catch her breath. Sirens blared, sounding a prolonged wail from behind the food tent. Flashing red lights cast a bright glow over the faces of the few people still gathered to watch. Two uniformed paramedics climbed out of the ambulance and approached Captain Cahill who had returned to supervise. Chris had gone off to interview other potential witnesses.

Kalina wrapped a comforting arm around her nephew and said, "AJ, I want you to call your mom and have her pick you up. You don't need to be here right now."

"What are you going to do?" His eyes glistened with unshed tears. He was trying to put on a brave face and it broke her heart.

"I'm going to have a talk with Mrs. Grant. Something about this whole situation seems strange."

"Aunt K., don't get involved. Please."

"I'll be fine. Now go call your mom."

AJ wandered off. Kalina headed for the beverage table and picked up two bottles of water before retreating to Mrs. Grant. Chris reached out a hand to bar her path. "Not everyone needs a chaperone to talk to me."

"I'm just bringing her some water. She looks like she could use it."

She sidestepped his outstretched arm and proceeded to sit down beside Mrs. Grant. The woman hadn't torn her gaze away from the corpse, even as the paramedics loaded her onto a gurney and rolled her to the back of the ambulance. Kalina was certain she'd be hit with her own wave of grief at the loss of her great aunt but for the moment, focusing on other people was keeping that feeling at bay. She would break down in private if she had anything to say about it. Kalina pressed an opened bottle of water into the woman's free hand.

"Mrs. Grant, are you all right?"

Finally, Mrs. Grant blinked several times and turned her attention to Kalina. "I'm sorry. What?"

"I just wanted to see if you were all right."

"Well, of course I'm not all right! My friend just died." Almost instantly, her demeanor changed. Her body sagged and she took a swig of water. "Sorry. I didn't mean to snap at you."

"I understand. Believe me. Can I ask you something?" The woman nodded and Kalina continued. "You said something earlier, right after Auntie Agatha died. You said that this couldn't be happening. What made you think that?"

Mrs. Grant took several long gulps of water and fussed with the hem of her blouse. "I ... I don't know what you mean. I suppose I was just shocked. It all happened so quickly."

"Kalina, that's enough. Go back to your booth and pack up like the captain said. Please." Chris ushered Kalina out of the tent and back to the promenade. She expected him to return to questioning witnesses but he kept a solid grip on her elbow all the way back to her booth

She pulled her arm free. "You don't trust me?"

"You always had a thing for sticking your nose in other people's business."

"Agatha is my family, Chris. If something happened to her, you can't expect me to just sit on my hands."

"Unless you joined the police force without any of us knowing, the best thing you can do is make sure AJ gives his statement while his memory is still clear. Okay?"

"You know I will."

Chris retreated from view. There was no way she was backing off now. Being back home had reignited a sense of loyalty she'd missed while being away. And she owed it to Auntie Agatha to find the truth. Whatever it may be.

3

Ten minutes later, Kalina stood by the car, loading the last box of merchandise into the back seat. AJ had disappeared again but she didn't have the heart to go find him. Settling the boxes so she could still see out the rear window gave Kalina a few private moments to let the reality sink in. The woman who'd been her confidante, her champion, was dead. Hot tears streamed down her cheeks and she barely kept a sob from passing her lips. She eased the back closed as her sister, Jillian, appeared from the gravel lot behind the refreshment tent. Her expression warned that she was not pleased. Jillian clearly hadn't heard the news. She stalked over to Kalina's car.

"What the hell is going on? You said you'd look after AJ for the day."

"Aunt Agatha is dead, Jill." Kalina dried her cheeks with the back of her hand.

"What? What happened?" Jillian demanded.

"I don't know. She was sitting having tea and then she just fell over I guess. AJ saw it happen and he's pretty freaked out about it. I figured you'd want him home with you guys. And the police have shut the fair down for the day."

"The police are involved?"

"I don't know that it's more than just an accident but they're looking into it. Chris wants AJ to give a statement down at the station."

"Chris?" His name caught her sister off guard.

"Detective Christian Harper."

Jillian let out a hiccup of laughter. "So you finally ran into the ex?"

"Yeah."

The levity vanished as Jillian collapsed against the hood of Kalina's car. "Aunt Agatha's really dead? Oh God. And AJ didn't say ... just to come pick him up."

Kalina pulled her older sister into a firm hug. "He'll be okay. He has you to lean on."

Jillian rubbed at her eyes to dry them and composed herself. "We just saw her a few days ago. God, it's like Dad all over again."

"We got through that. We're going to get through this, too," Kalina reminded her. They hadn't been the type of sisters who did everything together when they were kids but in that moment, Kalina felt like she was closer to her big sister than they'd ever been.

"You've always been the strong one, Kal," Jillian whispered as they stepped apart.

Kalina wasn't sure she agreed with her sister's assessment. "You'll need to make sure he goes down to the police station to give a statement. I promised Chris he would."

"I can do that. God, someone has to let Mom know. We'll have to plan a funeral and someone needs to clean out her house."

Kalina could hear her sister spiraling and she cut it off. "We will have time to do all those things. You need to be with your son now. Go."

Out of the corner of her eye, Kalina spotted Mrs. Grant making her way to the parking lot alone. "I have to go."

Without another word to her sister, she raced off in the hopes of intercepting Mrs. Grant. She had to jog to catch the older woman. "Mrs. Grant, can I offer you a ride home?"

"No. Thank you. I just want to be alone."

"I don't mind. Really. I was hoping we could talk without so many people around."

Mrs. Grant glanced around as if she feared they were being watched. "Tomorrow. Come by for morning tea."

"Thank you. I'll see you then."

It wasn't the sit down she'd been hoping for

but it would have to do. She couldn't explain why but she felt the need to go to aunt Agatha's house. Maybe it was because Jillian had mentioned it but maybe she just needed to feel close to her aunt one last time. The drive was short—less than twenty minutes and she pulled into the driveway. Agatha's car still sat there. She must have gotten a ride from Mrs. Grant to the fair.

Kalina may not have come to visit recently, but she knew her great aunt always left a spare key under the front mat. She bent down and flicked the top left corner down, finding the slender silver key where it had always been. She unlocked the front door and stepped into the front hall. She'd spent a lot of time in high school with her great aunt and she knew the layout like the back of her hand. She moved in the eerie silence to the bedroom first. It was empty, the bed made perfectly. Nothing felt off there and she retreated to the kitchen.

Everything looked in its place there, too. She had bowls from breakfast drying on the rack beside the sink. Her antique porcelain teapot sat on the stove ready for use. Kalina studied the pot and a memory flashed through her mind.

"You are going to do great things, Kali," Aunt Agatha said, pouring tea from the spout of the delicate pot.

"But, I've never been away from home this long before. And with Chris staying here, what if it doesn't work out?" She was seventeen, about to go of to college.

"The universe has a way of working things out. Keeping that balance. Whatever is supposed to happen will happen, my dear."

Kalina doubted that the sudden death of her aunt was in the universe's game plan. But maybe Chris stumbling back into her life was a sign. She pushed that thought away as she made her way into the living room. It was cozy with overstuffed couches and a recliner. The low table that stood in the center of the room bore something crumpled. It wasn't like Agatha to leave trash around. She bent and caught sight of typed text. Her whole body began to shake and she took a step back, pulling out her phone.

She dialed the only number she had for Chris and waited.

"Hello?" His answer sounded distracted.

"Chris, thank God you still have your old number. I'm at Aunt Agatha's house and I think there's something you need to see."

She retreated to the front steps to wait for his arrival. When he pulled up, he looked all business, badge clipped to his belt and a pair of latex gloves sticking out of his pocket.

"What are you doing here, Kal?"

"I just felt drawn here. But it's inside. Come on."

She led him to the living room and the crumpled piece of paper. He arched a brow in disbelief. "You brought me out here for a piece of paper?"

"She doesn't leave trash just sitting around."

He donned his gloves and smoothed out the page, revealing a single line of bold, capitalized text: **LYING IS A MORTAL SIN**. She looked at Chris after a beat. "Okay, that's cryptic."

Chris carried the note out to his car and slid it into a clear plastic bag marked 'Evidence'. Laying the bag on the passenger seat of his car, he turned and took her hands in his. Almost like he'd done the day he asked her to prom. "I know. But that's why I need you to keep out of it, okay? Let me do my job. Please, Kal."

The way he said her name, that small pleading note in it, tugged at heart heart. They may have grown up and apart but he was still the sweet boy who'd been her first kiss. Her first many things.

"Okay," she answered softly. He relinquished his grip on her hands and she spun on her heel, retreating to her car before he could say more. As she pulled out of the driveway, she wondered if Mrs. Grant knew about the note.

4

That night, Kalina couldn't sleep. The brief glimpse of Aunt Agatha's face —a twisted mask in death—invaded her dreams, waking her in cold sweats. She couldn't imagine how AJ was managing. Sure, she fancied herself a sleuth in theory, but maybe Chris was right. She wasn't equipped to handle dead bodies, especially when they were related to her.

"Don't focus on the dead," she mumbled to herself as the clock on her nightstand clicked over to two o'clock.

Kicking the sheets aside, she padded out to the kitchen to make a cup of coffee. If the day's events wouldn't let her sleep then she would embrace being the night owl. For a brief moment she wondered how superheroes like Daredevil managed to get any sleep with the nighttime crime fighting and a day job.

Settling in front of her laptop, steaming mug of coffee within reach, she logged on to the internet with the hopes of finding ... what exactly? For all of her progressive stances, Aunt Agatha had been a staunch opponent to social media. She'd insisted she didn't need everyone knowing all of her business. But she knew at least a few people who were frequent fair goers with accounts. And in a town as relatively small as Ellesworth, you were friends with everyone on Facebook. Small mercies. She logged on and scrolled through her news feed. Not surprisingly, lots of people had posted statuses from the Solstice Fair, often with accompanying photos. Photos were good. She scrolled through them all. Many were useless, images snapped at the top of the Ferris wheel or teetering over the first plunge on the roller coaster. But a few from folks her mother's age—yes, her mother had finally embraced the internet—had posted photos of some of the items they'd purchased and a few people had gotten shots of the pastry judging.

She let out a hiss between her front teeth at a not-so-flattering photo of Mrs. Grant laying into the judges. "Not a good look, Mrs. Grant."

What she needed was a shot of Aunt Agatha before her untimely demise. The refreshment tent boasted photo-worthy dishes. There had to be someone who had caught her in the tent before she died.

She lifted her mug to her lips but found the contents gone. The clock on her screen noted it was almost four in the morning now. She'd been scrolling for nearly two hours and found nothing. Barely stifling a yawn, she retreated to the kitchen for a refill. She'd look for another half hour and then try to get some sleep. She had a breakfast date with Mrs. Grant to keep, after all. Kalina slunk back into her chair and continued scrolling, the infusion of caffeine jolting her nerves and synapses awake. Just as the clock ticked from 3:59 to 4:00 she had a breakthrough. One of AJ's friends—Devon Landry—had a thing for food and had meticulously photographed the tent's contents. He'd also dragged AJ into a selfie. It wasn't much but she could make out Aunt Agatha sitting at the table behind them in the right corner of the picture. She clicked to the next photo in the album and nearly spilled her coffee down her shirt. Agatha lay on the ground and her body contorted mid-spasm. He'd photographed her death. She still didn't know for sure that her great aunt had been targeted, no matter what that cryptic note said. The last picture in the album depicted Aunt Agatha just before the paramedics arrive. Captain Cahill—at least Kalina assumed it was him from the back of his head—stood over her, shooing people away. Something about the scene gnawed at her mind. There was something to it. She just couldn't see what. Maybe Mrs. Grant would feel a little more forthcoming when the shock had worn off a little. Kalina downed the rest of the coffee and flopped onto the couch, hoping to get at least a couple hours of sleep.

"HELLO, MRS. GRANT? IT'S KALINA Greystone," she called through the screen door on Mrs. Grant's porch four hours later. She'd managed to sleep until seven.

No one answered. She waited before opening the screen door and knocking on the pale blue-painted wood behind it. Hand raised to knock a second time, Kalina stopped when the door eased open and Mrs. Grant appeared. Her eyes were red-rimmed and saucer-wide. The old woman hadn't gotten much sleep either.

"What are you doing here?" Mrs. Grant's gaze darted around as if she expected someone to jump out of the bushes.

"You invited me yesterday at the fair. And I didn't get my order of scones so I was hoping I could pick them up." Aunt Agatha would have insisted she keep her order.

Mrs. Grant peered around for another thirty seconds before she relaxed a little. Her shoulders rolled back and she stood up straighter. "Oh, yes. I nearly forgot. Please come in, my dear." She backed out of the doorway to let Kalina in. "And at least someone around here appreciates my baking."

Kalina didn't respond. She just followed the woman into her front foyer and took an immediate left into the living room. Mrs. Grant shuffled off to the kitchen without another word. Kalina took the time to check out the mantelpiece adorned with a simple silver urn at the center and a photo of a much younger Mr. and Mrs. Grant on their wedding day. She'd been to Mrs. Grant's house only a few times growing up, usually accompanied by Aunt Agatha. Kalina didn't have a very clear memory of Mr. Grant and in fact he'd rarely been around whenever she came by. But she didn't ever recall seeing an urn. A single framed photo of three women in their 30s sat on the other side of the urn. One of them was easily discernible as Mrs. Grant; the one in the middle bore a resemblance to Mrs. Davies and the third had to be Ms. Ellicott.

"Here we are. Do you take anything in your tea? I can never remember," Mrs. Grant reappeared with a tea tray.

"No, thanks." Kalina accepted the cup and saucer once Mrs. Grant had poured the tea. "When did your husband pass?"

"Alan? Oh, last year in a car accident."

"I'm so sorry."

Mrs. Grant glanced at the urn and gave a solemn nod. "It was a shock. But things like that always are."

Kalina took a sip of tea. "Like yesterday with Aunt Agatha."

Mrs. Grant fussed with her teacup, turning it one way and then the other atop the saucer. She wouldn't meet Kalina's gaze and, for longer than felt comfortable, she kept quiet. Kalina had time. She could be patient if that's what it took to make this woman open up about whatever she suspected.

"How are you and your family holding up?"

It was Kalina's turn to avert her gaze and contemplate the contents of her teacup. "I think we're all still in a bit of denial. I keep thinking we'll have to find her will, sort all of that out and then I shake my head because it just feels absurd. That she can't be gone."

"It's never easy when the loss is sudden," Mrs. Grant agreed softly.

Kalina took another sip of tea and cleared her throat. "I know you must still be processing what happened, too, but you didn't seem that surprised by what happened. If you think there's something else going on, you should tell someone. The police maybe."

"I don't know about that. What do I know? I'm just an old lady."

"But Aunt Agatha would want you to say

something. You were best friends," Kalina motioned to the framed photo on the mantle.

"Oh, we were. We'd grown up together, gone to school up through college and came back to Ellesworth after graduation. We met our husbands in the same circles. Goodness, that was a long while ago."

"I've seen you two. You were practically inseparable when I was growing up," Kalina pointed out. "That sort of friendship and loyalty runs deep. Please, if something did happen to her, I need to know. She was just as important to me as she was to you."

Mrs. Grant finally took a sip of her own tea and tears sprang to her eyes. "It just feels so empty without her."

Kalina nodded. "Believe me, I know. That's why I'm asking if you can think of anything that might have seemed off about her or anyone else. Did you see anything out of the ordinary after you left the pastry judging?"

"What do you mean?"

"I don't know. Was anyone paying more attention than usual to her?"

"Not that I recall. I mean she always had everyone swarming to place an order of her cake. It was just like every year."

Kalina pursed her lips, trying to figure out how best to phrase her question. "Did you notice if anyone went near her tea before she fell?"

"I wasn't paying attention. To be honest, I was just so upset about losing to that little..." Mrs. Grant took a long swallow of tea, cutting off the tirade.

"You're sure you didn't see anything at all? You didn't happen to notice if she made her own tea?"

"I think someone brought it to her maybe." Her brow furrowed. "Yes, I think someone brought it to her but I don't know who. Do they know what actually happened?"

Kalina shook her head. "I don't know." It did get her brain whirring. Agatha had been fine before the pastry judging and she'd only interacted physically with the judges long enough to accept her ribbon. And if, like Mrs. Grant and AJ said, she'd only had tea, then that seemed to be the logical delivery system if someone was in fact targeting her.

Mrs. Grant set her teacup down, hands trembling. She still wouldn't look Kalina in the eye. "It was lovely of you to stop by but I'm afraid I don't have time to visit any longer. Things to do."

Kalina didn't want to accept defeat but Mrs. Grant wasn't opening up like she'd hoped. She took her time finishing the cup of tea before standing up. "I appreciate your time, Mrs. Grant. When should I pick up those scones?"

"They should still have them at the fair. You can get them there." Mrs. Grant shuffled toward her as if to shoo her out of the house.

What was she hiding? Should she bring up the note she'd found in Aunt Agatha's house? It was a detail no one besides the police had right now "The police found a threatening note in Aunt Agatha's house. You wouldn't know anything about that would you?"

"N-no. I'm afraid not. I wish I could point you or the police to who would have wanted to hurt my friend, but I'm useless."

Kalina tried to give a sympathetic smile and offered the older woman a brief hug. "Thanks again for having me over."

Mrs. Grant shut the door behind Kalina, shoving her unceremoniously into the screen door. She let out a little grunt as the scratchy mesh snagged on her shirt and a loose wire scraped along her forearm. There was definitely something going on with Mrs. Grant. Just as she eased the screen door shut behind her, her phone beeped with a text message from AJ: "Can we talk?"

She sent back a quick note letting him know he could stop by the shop. In the meantime, she had some research to do and the shop was as good a place to do it as any.

5

It was a short trip from Mrs. Grant's house to Geeks and Things. Kalina pulled into the back lot and headed in through the game room, pausing to take in the new look of the space. It may not have been her first choice of dream job, but she knew she was far surpassing what her father would have expected of her. The shop was quiet as she settled behind the counter and pulled up a browser on her tablet. She stared at the search page that popped up, momentarily at a loss for what to do. If she was working off the theory that someone had intentionally targeted Aunt Agatha, then she just needed to figure out how they could have done it. The tea seemed the most efficient method. So, poison maybe? She typed in 'symptoms of poisoning' into the search bar and waited. The search engine helpfully populated the phone number for Poison Control as the very first entry. She scrolled through the thousands of results and was about to click on one just as the bell sounded above the door and AJ walked in. Dark smudges under his eyes and pale skin signaled he hadn't slept much the night before either.

"Hey. How you holding up?" She knew it was a redundant question given what had happened and his physical state but she couldn't help herself.

Her nephew hiccuped a breath and burst into tears. She laid the tablet aside and rounded the counter to fold him into a hug. "Shh. It's okay. You're going to be fine."

"I just feel so guilty. I should have done

something. CPR or I don't know. I shouldn't have just stood and watched."

"It happened so fast I don't think there was anything you could have done."

He sniffled and scrubbed at his tear-stained face with the backs of his hands. In that moment he was the little boy she'd babysat for on summers home from college, so young and vulnerable.

"Have you had your follow-up conversation with he police?"

"No. They called this morning and said that I needed to come down. They talked to Mom but it sounded serious. Can you come with me? Mom offered but I'd feel better if it was you. Besides, she's been super clingy since yesterday It's like she's afraid I'm going to kick it next."

"Sure. Let me just grab a few things."

She retrieved the tablet and keys, killed the lights and followed her nephew outside. The police station was only a five minutes walk from the shop and so they headed down the sidewalk side by side. Normally the fair would be rolling into day two but she assumed that given Aunt Agatha's death, it was cancelled. Aunt Agatha had been a fixture in the community. There would no doubt be an article in addition to the obituary for her but with so little to go on, even the hungriest of journalists wouldn't print anything just yet.

"Do you think the police think something might have happened to her? Like on purpose," AJ shoved his hands into the pockets of his shorts.

Kalina hesitated. She didn't want to speak for the police. There was every chance Chris had looked into the threatening note and discarded it. And she wasn't really supposed to have that information in the first place. "I don't know. Maybe. I'm sure if something did happen on purpose, they'll figure it out."

"Mrs. Grant seemed pretty upset yesterday," he offered.

"I went by this morning to see her. She's shaken up." She leaned in closer and whispered, "I think she might think someone was out to get Aunt Agatha. But she wouldn't say anything more. I'll figure out a way to get her to open up."

"Did you offer to buy her scones?"

"I did but that didn't work either," she said with a little laugh before sobering up. "I did find something at Aunt Agatha's house that might be fueling the police interest in her death."

"What?" Her nephew prompted.

"I really shouldn't be involving you," she said, trying to wave away his interest.

"What'd it say? Come on, Aunt K., don't hold out on me."

"Your mom wouldn't want me getting you involved in this."

"I'm already involved."

"Okay, fine. But this stays between us."

He gave a small fist pump in the air as the station came into view. "So, what did you find?"

"It was a note. It seemed out of place and it definitely was creepy. It said, 'Lying is a mortal sin.'"

They'd arrived at the station and Kalina held the door open for AJ to go first. The conversation died as soon as they crossed the threshold. Ellesworth PD was a small unit with about twenty uniformed officers, seven or eight detectives, one lieutenant, one sergeant and the captain. The precinct seemed strangely empty, especially if the fair had been called off for the second day, too. Chris sat at a desk studying a report. Kalina nudged AJ forward.

"Uh, Detective Harper, I'm here to give my statement," AJ said, inching closer to Chris's desk.

Chris jumped in his chair and gaped at AJ for thirty seconds before regaining his composure. Kalina settled in a seat at a vacant desk nearby. "I told you I'd bring him by today. I keep my word."

"I appreciate it." He sounded tired. Chris pushed the file aside and opened a document on his computer to start taking down AJ's recollection.

Kalina turned her attention to her tablet.

Luckily, the department was cheap enough not to password protect their Wi-Fi and she logged on to continue her internet search on poisons. She wasn't sure it would yield anything helpful but it was worth a shot. By the descriptions she found after clicking through a couple of sources, she was more convinced that this could be Aunt Agatha's cause of death. They all seemed to reference respiratory failure but the type of poison was less obvious. The coroner's office had probably done a toxicology report but those took weeks to come back, didn't they? And even though she was family, she wouldn't be privy to that information.

She was so lost in her thoughts she didn't notice the interview was finished until AJ snapped his fingers in front of her face. She blinked until he came into focus. He seemed relieved to have given his official statement. Kalina licked her lips and swallowed to dispel the cotton ball feeling in her throat.

"I'm all done. Do you want any help back at

the shop? Maybe figuring out what inventory to order?"

"Uh, yeah. Sure, that would be great."

She turned to thank Chris for his time but he'd disappeared. She fixed her nephew with a quizzical look but he just shrugged. The file Chris had been reading was still sitting on his desk. If he'd really wanted to keep her from snooping he would have put it in a drawer or somewhere less obvious and open. AJ said nothing as she crossed the short distance to Chris's desk and bent over the file.

Kalina was wrong. Apparently, Chris had specifically asked the lab to rush the toxicology report. Initially, she wasn't sure what she was looking at. The graph with thin spikes of different items in Aunt Agatha's blood was like reading a foreign language when you didn't know one word. She flipped through to a different page but it only listed a myriad of technical jargon.

"Uh, Aunt K., you might want to hurry. He's coming back."

Kalina glanced around but Chris was nowhere to be seen. Still, she trusted AJ not to let her down. She turned to the last page with the summary paragraph. Bingo! According to the test done, it showed thatAunt Agatha had high levels of inorganic arsenic in her blood at the time of her death. She had definitely been poisoned.

"Aunt K., come on," AJ hissed and made a move to tug her away from the desk.

She flipped the file closed and set it back on the desk where she'd found it. Exhaling a breath she hadn't realized she'd been holding, she and AJ headed for the front of the building.

"Hey, Kal," Chris said, appearing with a coffee cup in hand.

"Yes? Did you need me to give a statement, too?"

"No. I was just wondering, did I hear right that you're planning on running a game of Cards against Humanity at the shop?"

That was an awfully personal question for someone she hadn't spoken to in years. And he'd never exactly been the gamer type. Her cheeks flushed. "That's the plan, yeah."

"Well, count me in."

Either he'd developed a fondness for slightly inappropriate games or he was looking for a reason to see her. She couldn't deny that either option interested her. She nodded to show she

D heard his statement and turned around, wrapping a shaking arm around AJ's shoulders. She bit the inside of her cheek to keep from embarrassing herself. She hadn't ever thought she would be reconnecting with an old flame. They made it through the front door before her cell phone rang. The call ID said it was from the shop, which meant it was call forwarding.

"Hello, this is Kalina Greystone."

"This is Margaret Grant. I needed to tell you... Agatha wasn't the only one who got that note. I got one too."

6

Kalina stopped mid-step. Had she heard that right? Did she just get a break in this whole thing? It sure sounded like it. She forced her voice to work. "Oh. I can come right over."

"No, not here. The church down on Shore Drive."

"All right. I'll be there as soon as I can."

She ended the call and turned to AJ. "That was Mrs. Grant. She wants to talk."

"About what?"

"She said she got the same note I found at Aunt Agatha's house. This sounds like someone is targeting them. I just don't know why."

AJ turned back to the front doors of the police station. "Shouldn't you tell Detective Harper about this?"

"Not yet. I don't know what she knows. I don't want to waste his time if it's nothing."

"But she said she got one of those creepy notes."

"Saying it and meaning it are two different things. I'll let him know if anything solid comes out of this."

"Okay. What should I do now?"

"Go to the shop. I'll see you back there when I'm done."

They parted ways and, just as Kalina headed down Main Street toward the beach, she caught Chris watching her from a window. He just stared at her. She hoped he didn't try to follow her. She needed to find out if Mrs. Grant was telling the truth on her own. She needed to know she could do this.

The walk to Shore Drive was calming. It allowed Kalina to gather her thoughts and prepare for what she needed to ask Mrs. Grant. The Ferris wheel at the fairground rose up in the distance off to the right. She could imagine the workers starting to dismantle the machinery. Aunt Agatha's death had cast a pall over the festivities. She turned her attention to the simple, stone church up to her left. According to town history, it had stood since the 1700s. The interior had undergone renovation in the last few decades but the exterior stonework still held. She hadn't been inside since she was a teenager at AJ's christening. She didn't have anything against churches or organized religion but, as an adult, she didn't find faith particularly comforting or necessary to her life. But it was the perfect place for a confession.

Kalina blew out a breath as she eased open the doors to the narthex. She hadn't spotted Mrs. Grant's car but it wasn't that far of a walk, even for a woman in her 60s. The church was eerily silent. Despite being Sunday, services had been cancelled in order to help support the fair and the charity. She moved deeper into the sanctuary and spotted Mrs. Grant seated in the second pew from the front. Time to find out her secret.

"Mrs. Grant?" she called, not wanting to surprise the woman.

"Here, dear."

Kalina strode up to the front of the church and took a seat next to the older woman. They stayed quiet for a few moments, each taking in the image of Christ on the cross adorning the front of the pulpit. A powerful image for sure. The silence started to press on Kalina like a weight.

"You said you got a note too."

"Yes."

Kalina turned to sit sideways in the pew. "Did you bring it? Can I see it?"

Mrs. Grant opened her oversized purse and pulled out a folded piece of white paper. She started to hand it over but Kalina held up her hands. "I don't think I should touch it."

The older woman unfolded the page and held it up so that Kalina got a good look at it. **LYING IS A MORTAL SIN** was typed in bold caps just like the one she'd. Whoever had killed Aunt Agatha appeared to be targeting Mrs. Grant as well.

"When did you get it?"

"Last week. It just appeared under my front door, folded like that. I thought it was a flyer from one of the children or a reminder about the fair. I nearly had a heart attack when I saw what it was."

"Do you know who sent it to you?"

She folded the paper and shoved it back in her bag. "No. I don't. But the message seems pretty clear. And it scared me."

"Did Aunt Agatha get hers at the same time?"

"Maybe. She didn't say anything to me about it."

"Are you sure? Because it seems to me that whoever killed her might be coming after you too."

"She didn't say anything. And I mean what I said that I don't know who might have sent it. But... I might know what this is all about."

"Okay. Why don't you fill me in on what's going on?"

"There were three of us. A long time ago, thirty years or so, we did something"—she looked up at the crucifix—"unforgivable. There was a crime and someone went to jail. But ... it wasn't the right person."

"How do you know they weren't the right person?"

"Because we lied. We said we saw what happened but we didn't. Not as clearly as we thought we had when it happened anyway."

"So you filed a false police report."

Mrs. Grant shook her head and her eyes glistened with unshed tears. "We did more than that. We lied during the trial."

Kalina let that revelation sink in. Mrs. Grant, Aunt Agatha and someone else had committed perjury and sentenced an innocent person to prison. She didn't want to believe that the women were capable of such a thing. Aunt Agatha had been one of the most honest and trustworthy people Kalina had ever known.

"Are you absolutely sure you got it wrong? I don't believe that you'd do something like that. And neither would aunt Agatha," Kalina protested.

Mrs. Grant dabbed at the corners of her eyes. "Times were different. This town was different," she answered. It didn't explain anything.

As Kalina sat there beside the woman, she realized that whoever was targeting them had to know about the trial and the false testimony. But that could be anyone. And maybe this had nothing to do with the trial.

"Is there anything else that the note could be referring to?"

A single tear slid down Mrs. Grant's cheek. "No. I don't think so."

Kalina turned back to the front of the

church. A chill slithered down her spine as she considered her next question. "Who was the third person?"

"Cynthia Ellicott." Mrs. Grant's shoulders sagged but Kalina couldn't determine if it was relief or resigning her friend to the fear of being next on the killer's hit list. "But she won't talk to you. We had a bit of a falling out about a month ago. She got so mad at Aggie, I can't imagine she'd be happy to see her great niece show up on her doorstep."

Kalina couldn't imagine the trio falling out. They'd always been close and it didn't fit with what Mrs. Grant had told her the day before. Unless she was trying to avoid an argument from Aunt Agatha. Ms. Ellicott had babysat for she and Jillian when they were younger but her relationship to the woman hadn't gone much beyond seeing her at the fair in later years. "Thank you for telling me all of this. You should take that note to the police. They can keep you safe."

Mrs. Grant didn't respond to Kalina's suggestion. That was all right. She'd tip Chris off as soon as she got back to the shop. She needed an internet connection so she could do a little research on the trial. That was the key to finding the killer.

7

_K_alina made great time getting back to the shop. She pushed through the front door and stopped dead in the doorway. Chris stood at the counter, chatting with AJ about what looked like a video game. Both looked up when she entered.

"Hi, Kal." Chris waved.

"Hi. What's going on? I thought AJ gave you everything you needed and I didn't need to give a statement."

"This isn't official police business. This is a social call."

From behind the counter AJ gave her a wink and a quick thumbs up. *Brat!* Kalina was lost for words. One day back in each other's orbits and he was already making social calls. The high schooler buried deep inside her jumped at the potential for rekindling their romance. But they were such different people now; it couldn't be that easy to just fall back into each other's arms. *Could it?*

"I wanted to see what kind of games you had. See if any of them were appropriate for Jack and Benji."

"Um, okay."

It wasn't the way she wanted to break the news about what she'd discovered but it would have to do. There was the risk he'd berate her more in person as she couldn't just hang up, but it was one she had no choice but to take.

"Have fun," AJ said with a small wave.

Kalina led Chris back to the game room. She planned on getting more games as people requested them but she had a few staples that she'd picked up at a couple small conventions she'd attended. This wasn't exactly the venue she'd intended to share what she'd learned from Mrs. Grant but it would have to do. He browsed the table of games and picked up a small canister.

"Zombie Dice?" she said with a smile.

"Want to play?"

"This must be new. Like an uncle thing because you never used to like these kinds of games," she said but gestured to the table in the center of the room.

"They've grown on me,' he admitted with a sheepish grin.

"I have something to tell you," she broached, pulling out a chair.

"We can talk and play."

They settled across the table from each other and Chris went first. She wasn't paying attention to the dice as they skittered out across the table but she spotted the red shotgun blast. She was working herself up to telling him the truth.

"So I saw Mrs. Grant today."

"Oh?" He fished three more dice from the container and rolled them. She would have thought he would need an introduction to the game but he seemed quite competent.

"Well, she seemed so upset yesterday I wanted to make sure she was doing okay. She and Aunt Agatha were always so close. She was kind of like a de facto aunt, too."

"I guess you didn't forget your hometown manners being away in the big city."

"She told me something. She got a note just like the one I found at Aunt Agatha's house."

The dice slipped from his fingers and rolled both a green and yellow shotgun. His turn ended. "You shouldn't be digging into things. We've got it under control."

"She volunteered the information. What was I supposed to, just ignore her?" Kalina took her turn but didn't pay much attention to the outcome.

"So, are you sure she got one?"

"She showed it to me." She picked three more dice and rolled them. One shotgun and two brains. "I didn't touch it. I made sure not to."

"Where is she?"

"I left her at the church. You should send someone there and to her house to make sure she doesn't destroy it. Not that she would but ... just to be sure."

He pulled out his cell phone and sent a text. "Did she tell you anything else?"

"She said there might be a third person who got a note. Cynthia Ellicott. But I'm not sure. I guess she and Aunt Agatha had a falling out a few months back. So she might not be in the mood to talk."

"Did she say what the falling out was about?'

She picked up on his tone. He was slipping into interrogation mode. "No, she didn't. You don't think that Ms. Ellicott would hurt Aunt Agatha over an argument? I mean, she wasn't even at the fair. How could she possibly have done anything to..." She stopped short of saying 'poison her'. She wasn't supposed to know that information.

He held up his hands in surrender. "No, you're right. That doesn't make sense. But what makes Mrs. Grant think Ms. Ellicott might be a target, too?"

Kalina licked her lips. "She said they committed perjury thirty years ago."

"I should still speak to her, to confirm if she is indeed a target."

"I'd like to come with you."

"How many times do I have to tell you—"

"She might be willing to talk to both of us. If you just show up, it might spook her. Even if she wasn't on the best terms with Aunt Agatha, maybe she'll see me as a friendly face."

"You saying I'm not friendly?"

"No. But she used to babysit my sister and me when we were little."

"Fine. But you do exactly as I say, got it?"

"You have my word."

They left the table with dice spread across it and headed out through the front of the shop.

AJ leaned on the counter, his nose mere inches from his phone.

"Hold the fort," she called. A sense of unease settled on her as she followed Chris to his car. She hoped that Ms. Ellicott could shed some more light on this mystery.

8

Ms. Ellicott's house stood on the edge of the town away from everyone else. The more Kalina though about the woman the more she remembered her being kind of opinionated and irritable even as a younger woman. It was probably a good thing to be going as a pair to talk to her; Chris flashing his badge would only annoy her. Despite the summer warmth, the shutters were all closed on the front windows and the front door was shut. Stepping up onto the front porch, Kalina felt the tiny hairs on the back of her neck stand on end. Chris didn't appear to have the same reaction, or at least he hid it well. He yanked open the screen door and knocked sharply.

"Ms. Ellicott, this is Detective Harper with Ellesworth PD. I'd like to ask you a few questions."

No response. Kalina paced the length of the porch and noted the windows on both sides of the house were also closed up tight. "Maybe she decided to go on vacation."

Chris knocked again. "I don't think so." He pivoted and pointed to the car parked in the driveway. "Stay here. I'm going to check around back."

"Okay."

He jogged around the back of the house and Kalina tried the front door but found it locked. Standing there alone made her nervous. Something about this was wrong. Even people who didn't want to be around other people didn't shut themselves up like this. Not in this town. She abandoned the front of the house and made her way around the back, taking the same path Chris had to avoid spooking him. She hadn't seen a gun on his belt but that didn't mean he didn't have one concealed somewhere else.

"Chris?" she called out, hoping to give him even more warning that she was coming.

He didn't answer her and she picked up the pace. She rounded the back of the house and found him leaning against the side of the house bent double. The back door, which led to the kitchen, was open and a putrid smell wafted from the house.

"Oh God, what is that?" She gagged.

"We're too late."

Holding her breath, Kalina peered inside. Just within view, Ms. Ellicott lay on the floor with something silver protruding from her chest. There didn't appear to be much blood. She hoped the poor woman had gone quickly. For a split second, Cynthia's face vanished, replaced by Aunt Agatha and Mrs. Grant's. This could have been either of them. Her stomach churned and she backed away from the house, trying not to throw up.

"Do ... do you know how long she's been dead?"

Chris shook his head and coughed a couple times. "No. And being shut in the house like that is going to make it harder to figure out. I need to get a forensic unit down here."

"What should I do?"

His eyes watered, likely from the smell, and he pointed to the front of the house. "Go wait out front. Direct the EMTs when they get here."

"I can do that."

Chris pulled his phone from his pocket and hit a speed dial. "This is Detective Harper from Ellesworth PD. I need an ambulance to 1849 Spring Road. And I'm going to need a forensic team too. We've got another one."

Kalina retraced her steps back to the front of the house and took a seat on the front steps to wait. Someone was definitely targeting the women who'd lied at the trial thirty years ago. And they were succeeding in doling out punishment. She really needed to figure out who was after them. If she did, maybe she could prevent Mrs. Grant from being the last victim. A short time later, sirens wailed and an ambulance pulled to a stop in front of the house.

"Where are we going?" a male paramedic asked as he climbed out of the driver side.

"Straight back. She's in the kitchen."

She rubbed the back of her neck and waited for the forensic team to show up. She stared out at the trees and grass lining the street, anything to keep her from closing her eyes and seeing the dead woman inside the house. It was far worse than Aunt Agatha. Least her aunt had gone quickly. She had questions she wanted to ask but knew they couldn't be answered yet. Finally, a forensic van showed up and, just as the team disappeared toward the back of the house, Chris appeared.

"How are you holding up?"

"I don't know. I mean do you think if I'd told you sooner we could have stopped it?"

He sat beside her and wrapped his arm

around her shoulder. "I don't think so. Even without the heat of the house she's probably been dead at least a day."

Now she knew exactly how AJ felt witnessing Aunt Agatha's take her last breath. They sat together in silence and she leaned into his solid presence. She almost expected him to kiss her cheek reassuringly. But that was the thought of an enamored schoolgirl. She pushed down those feelings and squeezed her eyes shut to ward off tears. She needed to stay strong to solve this case. She owed it to Agatha and her friends, even if they had lied in the past. That didn't justify murder in the present.

"I know I'm not a cop but ... I feel like I'm a part of this case, Chris. Please don't keep me in the dark. I need to know what happened to them."

"I can't make that promise, Kal."

"You don't have to let me sit in on any interviews or anything, but what was it that killed her?"

"It looked like a letter opener."

"Did you find a note like the others got?"

"I don't know. Forensics is still working."

"Was it her letter opener?"

"I didn't get a good look at it."

"This has to be connected to that trial."

"Maybe. But forensics will do what they do and let me know what they find. As much as we want answers right now, we have to be patient. We want to make sure we have all the evidence to put whoever is doing this away."

"I know. I ... this is just scaring me a little. I come home and all of a sudden people are being murdered left and right."

"I'm pretty sure it wasn't you."

She smiled at him. "Thanks."

One of the forensic techs approached with two evidence bags in hand. One bore a white, printed piece of paper and even from this distance Kalina spotted the identical message. The second bag contained the letter opener. The silver handle bore what looked like a monogram etched into it.

"We found the note in the bedroom," the tech said.

"Okay. Let me see the weapon."

The tech handed over the letter opener and, for his part, Chris didn't stop Kalina from bending over to examine it with him. It was slender and the point was dulled with use. She tried not to look at the rust-colored stains marring the tip and half of the shaft. She'd been right about the top being monogramed. On closer inspection, she spotted an ornate "MG" embossed in flowery script underneath black fingerprint powder. She noted the swirls and whorls of an exposed print. She thought she spotted some blood on the sharp left point of the M but she didn't say anything. Pointing out evidence wasn't her job.

"I'm going to go out on a limb and say this wasn't hers," she said.

"I'm inclined to agree with you. Hopefully, the lab can identify whoever's fingerprint and blood that is."

She didn't want to say it but it looked like

the letter opener belonged to Mrs. Grant. It would explain why she'd been so reluctant to open up about the letter and the trial. Seeds of doubt took root in Kalina's mind. After all, with both Aunt Agatha and Ms. Ellicott dead, there was no one to confirm they'd in fact had a falling out. But she couldn't leap to conclusions just because the evidence was pointing in her direction. She would wait for proof before sharing her theory. Chris's phone beeped with a text message. He set the letter opener on the stair to his left and checked the screen. He frowned and rubbed at his temple.

"What's wrong?"

"I sent an officer to the church but Mrs. Grant wasn't there. She wasn't at her house either."

"Maybe she went back to the fairgrounds to help clean up."

"Yeah, maybe. I think I need to talk to her myself."

"If you don't mind, I think I'm going to head back to the shop and check on AJ."

"Good idea."

The paramedics rolled by with Ms. Ellicott on a gurney. The smell of death followed them and up close Kalina saw the fear etched into the woman's features. She didn't deserve to die. Not this way. Neither of them did. She pushed herself to her feet and raked a hand through her hair while she waited for the ambulance to pull away. Maybe they were lucky no one else lived close by. They didn't need people gossiping and spreading rumors. The ambulance eased back down the street without fanfare or sirens. They weren't keen to announce another death either.

"I guess we'll have to finish our game another time," Chris said as he placed a hand on her arm. "I've got to head back to the station and fill Captain Cahill in."

"Okay." Time for her to actually do that research she'd planned on.

9

———————

"Where'd you go?" AJ asked as soon as Kalina walked through the front door of the shop. She'd made a stop at home to pick up her laptop. She needed the extra processing power.

"You can't tell anyone but ... we found another body."

"Oh, crap. Who?"

"I can't tell you. Not if I want Chris to trust me enough not to leave me out of the loop going forward." She shut the door and flipped the sign to "Closed".

"Come on. You told me everything else. Maybe I can help."

"I appreciate it but this is more serious than we thought. I need you to go home."

"Please, Aunt K., let me help."

"I need to do this on my own, kid. Please just go home. I'm sure everything will come out when this is all over. But right now I don't need a sidekick."

"You know, the hero kicking the sidekick out never ends well," he muttered but took the back exit.

She felt a little guilty about booting him out of her research but she knew Jillian would never forgive her if he got mixed up with a killer—well, any more mixed up than he already was. But she would be the good aunt and do everything she could to protect her family. It seemed the killer had a specific target but she couldn't discount the possibility that he or she might lash out if the police closed in. She pushed those worries aside while she waited for her laptop to boot up and connect to the store's Wi-Fi. She navigated to the town's library webpage and searched for links to old newspaper articles. Unfortunately, it didn't look like they'd scanned all of the editions yet. They'd gone as far back as 1990 but she needed the 1980s. At the bottom of the list of available editions she saw a disclaimer that editions from the 1980s and earlier could be found at the library itself and the website offered a list of article titles from those editions. At least they were trying to be helpful.

Kalina typed in the search terms "trial" and "Cynthia Ellicott". She was the easiest to use because she'd never married so Kalina didn't have to worry about a name change after marriage. The page populated a list of results. There were a couple of articles in which Ms. Ellicott's name came up in connection with a trial. They were from the spring editions in March and April 1986. There was also an article from June 1987 linked to those from the year before. That was what she needed to find. She copied the article titles and editions and emailed them to herself, pulling the email up on her phone's email app before heading out to the library. She could feel a break in the case coming. Answers were almost within her reach.

A short time later, she sat in the newspaper archive section of the library in the basement. It was quiet and she was grateful for the solitude. She didn't need people asking questions she wasn't ready to answer. She started with the March editions, combing through the aged, brittle paper until she found what she was looking for. The article was buried within the third page and was shorter than she would have expected.

Local Man Charged with Murder to Stand Trial

By: Adam Jenkins, Staff Reporter

It was a quiet night on February 18, 1986 when the authorities were called upon to investigate the body of a young girl found down near the waterfront. The victim, later identified as 16-year-old Alice Beech, appeared to have sustained injuries consistent with a physical assault, according to police who were on scene. The case developed no leads as Alice's family begged the townspeople for someone to come forward. They offered a reward for any information leading to the capture of their daughter's killer.

A break in the case came as blustery February turned into March. Three witnesses, including Ms. Cynthia Ellicott, came forward stating that they had been out for a walk on the beach when they observed a car speeding away toward the center of town. According to their statements, the vehicle passed by street lights illuminating the face of the driver. The suspect, identified as Samuel Gordon, 31, was arrested at his home on March 9, 1986 and he has been indicted on charges of murder. A trial is expected to commence on March 24th in the Salem County Courthouse. Gordon remains in custody as bail has been denied.

According to sources, Gordon has relatives out of state and the judge believes him to be a flight risk. At this time it is unclear whether Ms. Ellicott and the other witnesses will testify at trial.

Kalina leaned back and let out a breath. She'd been a toddler when Alice Beech died. No one in town liked to talk about it. In fact, she couldn't even recall the case ever coming up after church on Sundays when she was young. And those ladies always liked to gossip. She checked the list on her phone again for the next article. It came from the April 10th edition. This time Mr. Jenkins made the front page with a faded color photo of the defendant sitting in court. He looked vaguely familiar, which was ridiculous. She'd never met the man. This article was also short on detail. Apparently Mr. Jenkins and his editor believed in brevity.

Gordon Trial Drags On, Public Restless for Result

By: Adam Jenkins, Staff Reporter

Trial is still underway at the Salem County Courthouse. The prosecution's case closed on Friday. Defendant Samuel Gordon has yet to take the stand and reports indicate he may not testify in his own defense. While he is not required to do so, there is no doubt the jury will consider it a strike against him.

Perhaps the highlight of the prosecution's case came when Ms. Cynthia Ellicott, 30 and two other witnesses testified as to their recollections of the night in question. Ms. Ellicott testified that she, "saw a man driving away very fast from where poor Alice was found." Ms. Agatha Hammersmith testified that, "Yes, I'm sure it was the defendant who killed that poor girl," and when asked how she knew this, replied, "I saw his eyes. I could never forget the look of madness in them." Finally, Ms. Margaret Cook testified that she, "recalled the license plate of the car and it matched the car driven by the defendant."

Public sentiment is clear. They want a conviction sooner rather than later. Alice's parents asked the defendant to simply confess to the crime so they could let their daughter rest in peace.

It definitely seemed like Mrs. Grant, Aunt Agatha and Ms. Ellicott had been sure of what they'd seen. It also appeared that Mr. Jenkins was very pro prosecution. He'd barely afforded Mr. Gordon any humanity. Even if he was guilty of the crime, he was still a person who' was supposed to be innocent until proven guilty. Kalina had no way of knowing which details were fabricated but she was beginning to sus-pect most of them had been made up. Perhaps someone in the police force had pressured them to make statements against Sam Gordon. Or perhaps the real killer had threatened them for their perjured testimony. There were two more articles on the list. She had to retrieve a new set of editions from the shelves to find the one from April 18th. Again, Mr. Jenkins made the front page. This time the photo depicted Sam Gordon, face in his hands. The article was a short paragraph.

Gordon Sentenced to Life

By: Adam Jenkins, Staff Reporter

After an abbreviated defense, in which counsel for the defendant, Alan Grant, did not question anyone but Gordon's wife, Catherine, to attest to his character, the jury retired for the shortest deliberation in the history of Ellesworth. Only ninety minutes after being issued jury instructions, they returned with a verdict: guilty. Gordon was sentenced to life in prison for Alice Beech's murder. He was seen crying as the bailiff removed him from the courtroom. He was not permitted to say goodbye to his wife or son.

Kalina let out a gasp and a single tear ran down her cheek. She was beginning to understand why someone would want revenge on the people who led to the wrongful conviction and imprisonment of this man. As she dried her eyes and returned the newspaper to its protective folder, she had to wonder. Why had Gordon's lawyer not let him testify? Surely he had an alibi? Why did the attorney not cross-examine the witnesses? Had the attorney had something to do with setting Gordon up? She scanned the article one last time before she put it back.

"Oh damn!" She bit her tongue for swearing but there was no one around to hear her.

The pieces were starting to come together. She had to check one piece of information but she had an idea why the three women were involved. She still had one final article, from June 1987, to review and it didn't make sense to abandon the newspaper archives until she'd done so. The final article was even shorter than the one about the verdict.

Murderer Samuel Gordon Takes Own Life

By: Adam Jenkins, Staff Reporter

In what can only be deemed a further admission of guilt, one year and two months after he was sentenced to life in prison for the brutal murder of Alice Beech, Samuel Gordon was found dead in his cell. Reports confirm he hung himself. Gordon is survived by his wife Catherine and their son, Danny. Unable to take the shame, Catherine and her son moved out of the area. It is rumored she now goes by her maiden name.

"Well, that's as clear a motive as you're likely to get," she said to no one in particular.

She needed to go check marriage records. If she could figure out what the former Mrs. Gordon changed her name to, she might have a better shot at pointing Chris in the right direction. Her phone buzzed with an incoming call. There was no Caller ID.

"Hello?"

"Kal, it's Chris Harper."

"Hi. Is something wrong?" She almost felt guilty for using her phone in the confines of the library. Almost.

"I wanted to let you know that the lab put a rush on that fingerprint on the letter opener."

Kalina's heart started to race at the unexpected news. He was keeping his word about looping her in on the investigation. Maybe she could point out that she had discovered the motive for the killings. "Who does it belong to?"

"You aren't going to like it. It matched Margaret Grant."

She let out a groan. "No, that can't be right."

"Well, I'm afraid it is. I mean, come on. It was monogramed with her initials."

"But you don't know that it was hers. Plenty of people in town have those initials."

"Name one."

"I... I can't think of anyone off the top of my head. But, Chris, I think I found something. Have you looked into the trial angle?"

Muffled sounds came over the line. "Believe me, we're following all the leads. I have to go. Officers just brought Mrs. Grant in. They found her at the cemetery visiting her husband. I just wanted you to know."

He hung up before she could share the news that, even if the evidence pointed to Mrs. Grant, the poor old woman was being framed. Just like Sam Gordon. She rose halfway out of her chair and stopped. Should she finish up here or go and try to observe the interrogation? Was that even possible? She didn't have time to debate. If she didn't move fast, the wrong person would be arrested for a crime they didn't commit—again.

10

───────

Kalina hastily put the newspapers back in their respective bins and took the stairs to the main level of the library two at a time. Pushing the front door open in a hurry, she staggered as the summer heat smacked her in the face. Sweat prickled along her hairline and her upper lip. She hadn't noticed how cool the basement had been. The sudden change in temperature only spurred her on to get to the police station.

By the time she arrived, she felt as if she'd been dunked in salt water. A quick glance in the mirror in the women's bathroom dispelled the idea that she was drenched in sweat. The central hub of the station was still sparsely populated, save for the two uniformed officers. They looked like they were right out of the academy, maybe only a few years older than AJ. They were both staring at a TV monitor that looked like it belonged in the early 1990s. At least it was in color and the audio seemed to be working. Mrs. Grant sat on the far side of a rickety-looking, faux wooden table. Chris sat across from her with a bulging folder. Kalina inched closer to better hear the conversation.

"Mrs. Grant, are you sure you don't want a lawyer present?"

"If I really needed one, you would have told me that you're charging me with something."

"Ma'am, I need you to affirmatively state that you are waiving your right to have counsel present during this interview."

Mrs. Grant pressed her lips together and squared her shoulders. "I do not want a lawyer. Is that clear enough for you?"

Chris coughed. "Yes, thank you. Now, I'd like to talk to you about Cynthia Ellicott."

"What about her?"

"You two are friends?"

"I suppose."

"In fact, you were friends with both Cynthia and Agatha weren't you?"

"Yes. What does that matter?"

"You know that Agatha died at the fair. We discovered Cynthia Ellicott's body earlier today in her home. She'd been stabbed—" he retrieved the bloodstained letter opener, still safely sealed in its evidence bag "—with this."

Kalina waited for Mrs. Grant to react. The older woman studied the letter opener through the clear plastic in silence for what seemed like hours. Finally, she let out a shudder and dabbed at her eyes.

"That's terrible."

"Have you seen this letter opener before?"

"I don't know. Why should I have?"

"We lifted a fingerprint from the handle." He pointed to the swirls of fingerprint powder still clinging to the metal. "It was a match to you. So would you like to rethink your answer?"

Mrs. Grant kneaded her hands together in a nervous tic. She glanced around the small interview room, anywhere but at Chris. "I leant that to Cynthia ages ago. She never returned it. She was always forgetting to give things back even when we were girls in school."

"When was the last time you saw her?"

"Last week. I cooked for her a few times a week. Those awful frozen meals were no good for her health."

"When was the last time Agatha saw her?"

"A month or two ago. They had a falling out."

"Over what?" Chris prodded.

"Neither of them wanted to tell me."

"But you knew them both well. Couldn't you guess?"

"You're right, I knew them well. Which means I knew not to press when they didn't want to talk about it." She rubbed at her upper lip, her gaze darting to the letter opener again.

"You can't honestly believe I would murder my friends. That's lunacy!"

Chris didn't respond. Instead, he reached into the folder again and produced one of the notes. Kalina couldn't tell which one it was. They'd all looked identical. Chris pushed the evidence across the table to Mrs. Grant. "Do you recognize this?"

"Someone slipped it under my door."

"When?"

"I don't remember. Last week maybe."

"Last week or you don't remember, which is it, Mrs. Grant?"

She fidgeted and kneaded her hands again. "Last week."

"When you went over to Ms. Ellicott's house, did you talk about the note?"

"No, it didn't come up."

Kalina chewed her lower lip. She didn't like where this was going. Sure, the evidence looked bad but she knew the reason. Someone was framing Mrs. Grant. She needed to get that information to Chris before he made a huge mistake.

"Okay, let's talk about Samuel Gordon," Chris said, her words freezing Kalina in place.

"I don't want to talk about him," Mrs. Grant said.

"I'm aware that all three of you testified in his trial thirty years ago."

"Well it wasn't a secret," she murmured.

"No, but you didn't tell the truth back then, did you?"

He really had looked into the trial like Kalina had suggested. She was rooted to the spot, waiting to hear what Mrs. Grant said. "You talked to Aggie's niece I take it."

"It's my job to look into every possibility and trust me, she's a smart woman."

Kalina smiled in spite of the situation. Still, she needed to share the pieces that were coming into focus. She cleared her throat and caught the attention of the rookies watching the interrogation.

"Can we help you?" One of them asked.

She gestured to the monitor. "I need to talk to Detective Harper about the murders of Cynthia Ellicott and Agatha Davies. Tell him it's Kalina."

The one who'd spoken to her scurried off and moments later appeared on the screen. He bent down to whisper in Chris's ear. Chris stood and addressed Mrs. Grant. "Excuse me. I'll be right back."

he appeared in the bull pen and gestured for her to follow him back to his desk. The other officers eyed them but didn't intervene.

"What are you doing here, Kal?"

"You called me, remember?" She noted. he fixed her with an irritated look. "I have a theory about what's going on and I thought you should know."

"I thought we agreed you'd leave the police work to me."

"You're going to get it wrong if you just follow what the evidence says."

He grabbed her by the elbow and ushered her into Captain Cahill's empty office. "Tell me why I shouldn't follow the evidence, then."

"You already know about Sam Gordon's trial. I read the news articles from back then. They weren't very favorable to him. The coverage of the trial was sparse, which seems kind of weird. And Mrs. Grant admitted to me that she and the others lied during the trial. I think someone involved in the case somehow is coming back to get revenge."

"Targeting the witnesses," Chris murmured.

"Not just the witnesses. Mrs. Grant's husband was Sam's lawyer. He did a shoddy job defending him. And Mrs. Grant told me he died a year ago in a car accident."

"That's right. Pretty nasty scene from what I heard. Slammed into a tree," Chris explained.

"When last year?"

"I don't know. Summertime."

"June?"

"I would have to double check but that sounds about right."

"What about the reporter, Adam Jenkins?"

Chris' brow furrowed. "Hang on." He stepped out of the room and spoke quietly with one of the rookies. Kalina watched him move to a computer and begin typing. Minutes later a sheet of paper spat out at a nearby printer and Chris retrieved it. He returned back to the captains' office and held out for Kalina to see. Adam Jenkins had suffered a heart attack back in April.

"Whoever this is is smart. They're making it look like accidents and they're framing the rest of the people involved," she said.

"I promise, we're going to do everything we can find out who is behind this."

She headed for the front door and caught sight of one of the new officers coming out of the interview room looking shell shocked. He approached Chris and said, "She wants a lawyer."

"Go home, Kal. There's nothing more you can do here. I promise as soon as we crack this case and have the killer in custody, I will personally let you know," Chris said. The way he pressed his hand to her arm and leaned forward suggested he wanted to do more than just usher her out the door.

If she could figure out one final piece of information she could finally solve this puzzle.

11

———————

Kalina's nerves tingled as she jogged back to the shop. She could do her last bit of research there. The records she needed were electronic, even that far back. She hoped it would take a little while for Mrs. Grant to get her lawyer. It would give Kalina the time she needed to figure out who the real killer was and, hopefully, allow Chris to catch them before any more lives could be ruined

"We're closed," AJ called when Kalina tried the front door.

"AJ, it's me! Let me in."

The lock released and her nephew appeared in the doorway. "Sorry."

"I thought I sent you home," she chided and pushed past him.

"You did. I didn't listen. What did you find out?"

"I'm not sure I should tell you."

"I'm not a little kid anymore. I can handle it."

"No. I'm not going to be responsible for putting you in therapy. You can stay but only if you go clean up the game room."

He rolled his eyes. "I wasn't even the one who made the mess."

"And yet I'm the boss and I say go clean it up."

"Fine."

She swatted his arm as he walked by. Now alone in the front of the shop, she grabbed her tablet and fired up the library website. The town was small enough that the library housed most of the town hall records regarding marriages, births and deaths. She found the listing for marriage licenses and typed in Samuel Gordon. With any luck he'd be the only one in town. It seemed luck was on her side. There was a single entry for a Samuel Gordon dated February 9, 1975. There was a scanned-in version of the actual license and she opened it up in a new tab. She had to enlarge the picture to get the image clear enough to read.

The tablet fell out of her hands and clattered on the counter. It couldn't be right. Taking two deep breaths, she picked up the tablet again and looked. She'd been right the first time. Samuel Gordon had married one Catherine Cahill. Her stomach sloshed, suddenly uneasy, as she navigated to birth records and typed in Daniel Gordon. Sure enough, a record appeared from April of 1976. Daniel Michael Gordon had been born a healthy little boy to Samuel Gordon and Catherine Gordon.

Kalina slumped against the countertop, her

ears ringing with the realization of what it all meant. How could she have missed it? The last article had practically screamed the information at her! But she needed to be sure. The phrase the three women had been sent was very specific. Something deep down in her mind insisted she had to be absolutely sure of the killer's identity before she started accusing people. Chris wouldn't believe her unless he had actual proof.

Swallowing several times so she could speak, she dialed Chris' number and waited. It rang three times. Four. Five. Finally, just before it flipped to voicemail, he picked up.

"Hey, we're still waiting for her lawyer."

"I uh..." Her voice shook.

"Is everything okay?"

She should tell him what she'd found but she couldn't get the words out. "Yeah, fine. I just... I needed to know something. Where did you say the officers found Mrs. Grant?"

"The cemetery. Why?"

"No reason. I was just wondering. I have to go."

She hung up before he could question her further. Did Mrs. Grant have it figured out too? Or did she just want to pay her respects and voice her apology to the man she and her friends had pushed to an early grave? Either way, she needed to find that gravesite. With a quick glance toward the back room, she rushed out through the front door. AJ could handle himself.

The cemetery was on the other side of the church. Mrs. Grant probably hadn't left the area after they'd spoken. By the time she reached the main gate, Kalina's calves had cramped from running and her chest burned from the stress of the run. She wasn't out of shape by any means but the whole situation was taking a toll. As she eased through the gate and began searching the stone markers, she wondered how it could have only been two days since Aunt Agatha died. It was clear that

Ms. Ellicott had, in fact, been the first victim. An involuntary shiver danced down her spine. Nothing like this was supposed to happen in Ellesworth. It was just a sleepy, little coastal town with nice people.

The headstones varied in color, some brand new, others beaten down and almost illegible with age. She longed for a helpful "You Are Here" map but was left to wander aimlessly through the rows of the dead. She had nearly reached the back fence when she spotted what looked like fresh flowers leaning up against a slightly weathered headstone. They looked familiar somehow. Kalina's heart sank when she reached the stone to find it belonged to none other than Samuel Gordon. He'd been buried at home after all. The epitaph read, "Lying is a mortal sin and you never did." She had all the proof she needed now. She snapped a photo of the grave and sent it off to Chris with a message that she had found the proof that Mrs. Grant was being framed. And the flowers finally clicked in her addled brain. Captain Cahill had given the same flowers to Leslie when she won at the fair the day before. Now she just needed to get to the station and warn Chris about Captain Cahill before it was too late.

12

———————

This time, Kalina really was drenched in sweat as she staggered through the front door of the police station. Chris hadn't responded to her text but she hadn't really expected him to. The station was eerily empty and quiet. Where was everyone? She moved slowly, afraid something or someone might jump out at her at any second. The tiny hairs on her arms stood on end, another warning sign. She finally reached the monitor linked to the interview room. Mrs. Grant still sat there, alone, a plastic bottle of water cupped between her hand. Where was her lawyer? She'd asked for one nearly an hour ago. And where was Chris?

"Hello?" she called out.

No response. This wasn't right. She studied the video feed and noted that the folder of evidence was no longer strewn across the table. It didn't explain why Mrs. Grant had been left alone. Kalina's stomach churned again and she swallowed back the rising acid. She fished her phone from her pocket and dialed Chris's cell phone. This time it rang five times before clicking over to voicemail.

"Chris, this is Kalina. I don't know where you are but I figured it out. Please call me back."

Her palms turned slick with sweat as she ended the call and the phone slid from her fingers, clattering to the floor. She bent to pick it up and stopped with her fingertips brushing the screen. The front door squeaked open. The irrational part of her brain told her it was Cahill and he had come to finish what he'd started. Her heart began hammering in her chest and the blood rushed in her ears, drowning out all other sound. Balancing with one hand on the floor, she swore she felt vibrations as someone walked into the room. The vibration intensified and then stopped.

"Kalina? What are you doing?" Chris offered his hand.

Forgetting her phone for the moment, relief washed over her. She allowed him to pull her up and she collapsed into his arms. He staggered back a step under her weight before he eased her into a chair and retrieved her phone for her.

"You look pretty freaked out," he said.

"Why is Mrs. Grant in there alone?"

"It's taking her lawyer longer to get here than we thought."

"I texted you, why didn't you answer?"

"I was chasing down some other evidence. I think you might be right and Mrs. Grant is being framed. There are some inconstancies in the evidence that don't fit."

"So why is she still sitting here? You should let her go."

"I still have to follow protocol."

"I know who the real killer is. We need to get Mrs. Grant somewhere safe."

"I don't know how many more times I have to say it. I'm on this."

"You aren't listening to me. The killer is—" she began but he held up a hand.

"I don't need your speculation. Come on, I'm taking you home. No more digging into things."

He didn't give her a choice as he dragged her out of the station and into his car. She caught movement out of the corner of her eye but Chris pulled out of the small lot and onto Main Street before she could get a good look.

13

"Who did you send to watch Mrs. Grant?" Kalina's throat felt raw.

"Everything will be fine. The captain is on it. He won't let anyone near her."

Kalina's whole body went numb. In a foolish move she reached for the steering wheel, anything to get Chris to stop the car. Panic flushed his face and he slammed on the breaks. The car narrowly avoided plowing into a mailbox. She was going to regret that action.

"What the hell are you doing? You could

have killed us!" His voice echoed in the confines of the car.

"I'm sorry but you can't leave her with him. She won't be safe."

"Why not?"

"Because he's the killer!"

Her declaration hung in the air between them for far too long. She tugged on the seatbelt release but it wouldn't unlatch. Chris stared at her, mouth hanging open in obvious disbelief. She could tell he was trying to find words but they wouldn't come. Finally, the seatbelt unhooked and slid with a sharp 'zip' back to its original position.

"What... I don't understand."

"Sam Gordon, the man who killed himself, had a son named Daniel. After Gordon killed himself, his wife and son left town and started going by her maiden name, Cahill. It's all in the town records. I don't think that Alan Grant's accident was an accident. Or that Adam Jenkins really had a heart attack. And I bet you Cahill was on the scene for both. We have to go back before he finishes what he started."

Chris continued to stare at her, taking the information in. She needed to act, to turn the car around and get back to the station. She snapped her fingers in front of his face; it did nothing to rouse him from his trance. Finally, the blare of a nearby emergency vehicle snapped him out of his shock. An ambulance flew past them in the direction of the police station.

"Put your seatbelt back on," Chris ordered before he gunned the engine and the tires squealed on the pavement as he turned the car to follow the path of the flashing lights.

Kalina didn't have time to bother with the seatbelt. She gripped the edge of the passenger seat and braced herself against the door as Chris employed driving skills better suited to a race-car driver than a mild-mannered police detective. They rolled into the station's parking lot maybe two minutes after the ambulance. Two paramedics—not the ones who had been

on scene for Aunt Agatha or Ms. Ellicott—
jumped out of the rig and raced through the
front door with medical bags slung over their
shoulders.

"I need you to stay out of the way," Chris
said and shoulder-checked his door open.

"Yeah, okay," she replied and followed suit.

She could stay out of the way and still see
what was going on. She flashed to all kinds of
horrible scenarios in the thirty seconds it took
them to get inside. She imagined Mrs. Grant
lying on the ground stabbed to death like Ms.
Ellicott. The reality was worse. The camera
feed to the interview room was still active. A
man who looked to be in his forties sat on the
floor cradling Mrs. Grant's head in his lap. The
paramedics ordered him to stay out of the way
as they checked for a pulse and an airway.

"Just like Aunt Agatha," Kalina whispered
just loud enough for Chris to hear.

"You don't know that."

"Chris, the water. You have to tell them it
was arsenic."

"How do you know about that?"

"I saw the report on your desk. Look, yell at me later. She's going to die!"

Chris waved a hand at her to shut her up and took three long strides to the open doorway to the interview room. "She may have been poisoned with arsenic."

One of the paramedics nodded and started to do chest compressions. His partner held Mrs. Grant's limp wrist lightly between his fingers. "I've got a pulse. We need to move."

Kalina and Chris backed out of the way as the medics loaded Mrs. Grant onto a gurney and raced with her out the front doors of the building. Sirens wailed as the ambulance took off. Kalina had no idea if time was on Mrs. Grant's side or not. She hoped they wouldn't have to bury three people at the end of this. The man who had been in the interview room —she assumed he was Mrs. Grant's attorney— dragged himself to a standing position and looked around dumbfounded. Chris closed the distance and leaned in close.

"What did you see? What happened?"

"I don't know. I got a call that Margaret needed an attorney. I was with my son and daughter. I had to find someone to watch them. I came as soon as I could. When I got here she was slumped over in the chair. So I called 9-1-1."

Chris ran a hand through his hair and let out a frustrated breath. "You didn't see who brought her the water?"

"No. I'm sorry. I should go to the hospital."

Chris dismissed him with a wave of his hand and the lawyer moved with brisk steps until he disappeared from view. Kalina studied the empty station in shock. What were they supposed to do now? They knew that they needed to find Captain Cahill but where to look? A single 'beep' punctured the silence between them. Chris glanced at his phone and tapped the screen a couple times.

"Damn it!"

"What is it?"

"DNA came back. There were minute traces of blood on the letter opener that didn't belong to Cynthia. You were right. It belongs to Captain Cahill. And the only prints on the teacup belonged to Agatha and the captain."

"Chris, I'm so sorry." She wasn't sure why she said it but it felt like the right thing to say.

His facial features hardened into a mask of determination. "You don't have anything to be sorry for. If it weren't for you pushing me, I'd be slapping cuffs on the wrong person."

Before she could respond, one of the fresh-faced officers wandered in. "Sir, what's going on?" His voice shook with nerves.

Kalina stepped out of Chris's orbit. The officer was in for an interrogation of his own. Chris launched himself at the kid and grabbed the front of the officer's uniform in his fists. "Who gave Mrs. Grant that bottle of water?"

"I ... don't know what you're talking about."

Chris dragged the officer into the interview room and shoved the man's face to within a few inches of the bottle. "This one. Who gave it to her?"

"I did. She said she was thirsty."

"Where did you get it?"

"The fridge. What's going on? Where's the witness?"

"You poisoned her," Kalina said in a soft tone.

The officer blanched. "What? No I didn't. I just ... gave her water."

"She's on her way to the hospital. She didn't look good when he left here," Chris said, his tone sharp.

"Chris, I don't think he had anything to do with this. We should be focusing on finding the captain." She walked into the room and placed a hand on Chris's bicep, trying to exude calm.

Chris's entire body tensed under her touch. Slowly, second by second, he relaxed and released his grip on the officer. The officer leaned against the table, clearly afraid of another outburst. Without realizing it or intending to, Kalina slid her hand down Chris's arm and took him by the hand, leading him back into the open space of the station.

"We have to find him," Chris said.

"I know. Can you ... I don't know, track his phone or something?"

"You're brilliant." Chris pulled her into a one-armed hug and planted a kiss on her cheek as he dialed a number on his phone. "This is Detective Chris Harper out of Ellesworth PD. I need a trace on a phone."

Kalina didn't hear him rattle off the captain's number. She was too focused on the kiss. Maybe there was something left between them. Two minutes later, Chris ended the call and rounded on the officer who had slowly inched his way out of the interview room. "You need to get your partner and follow me. No lights or sirens. We are going in quiet."

"Where are we going?" Kalina asked.

His phone beeped twice at him and he opened a map app. A tiny red dot blinked from the middle of the screen. "The cemetery. Let's go."

14

———————

Kalina sat in the passenger seat of Chris's car in silence. She stared ahead at the road in front of them, leading to the cemetery and the church. They could have walked it from the station but Chris insisted on driving. Maybe he needed to feel in control of the situation. She didn't argue. She was just grateful he was letting her come along. It had to be violating who knew how many rules to have a civilian involved in an arrest like this. She was also surprised that Chris only had the two new officers for back up. He pulled the car into a spot near the front gate and cut the engine. The car clicked and rattled as the engine block cooled. He turned to her but she held up a hand to silence him.

"I know. Stay out of the way. I got it. I'm not stupid or a hero. This is your show."

"Thank you. I mean it."

"Thank me when this is all over."

He quirked a half-smile at her before easing the driver side door open and shutting it as quietly as possible. The two uniformed officers climbed out of the cruiser beside them. Chris removed his gun from its hip holster and the other officers followed suit. Chris consulted his phone before stepping through the open gate.

"The grave is near the back fence on the far right," Kalina offered in a whisper.

Chris pointed at each officer and then to the left and the right of the cemetery. They were going to surround Captain Cahill. He might try to jump the fence but it was wrought iron and spiked at the top. There wasn't much chance he would make it over before Chris or the other officers got to him. Chris let them go first before he started forward, gun gripped in his right hand but down by his thigh. Kalina stayed behind him a few paces, just as she'd promised.

The cemetery felt strange as they moved through it. It hadn't held any special meaning for Kalina before, but now—even with all the other people around—she felt the quiet awe and respect for the dead one should have upon entering this place. And she could swear she felt a touch of sadness for Sam Gordon's fate. She thought she might feel a little sliver of empathy for Captain Cahill but she didn't. He may have been acting out of a place of love for his father but his actions were inexcusable.

They reached the back fence and found the captain kneeling in front of his father's grave, rearranging the bouquet of flowers. The uniformed officers hung back just out of sight, weapons at their sides. Chris motioned for Kalina to stay where she was as he took a few steps closer to the headstone. He still held his gun against his thigh. He made sure to step on some loose twigs.

"Captain," he called.

Captain Cahill turned to face them. He didn't look surprised. Had he really expected they would catch him? He stayed crouched down but pulled his hands away from the flowers. He held them out, fingers splayed in a gesture that Kalina assumed meant he was unarmed.

"Sir, I'm going to need you to pull the weapon out of your ankle holster and toss it to me," Chris instructed.

With slow movements, Captain Cahill complied. Chris bent down, scooped up the gun and tucked it into his waistband. Dead air filled the space between the two cops; neither seemed to know what to say. Kalina longed to speak, to say she understood why Cahill felt betrayed, but that wasn't her job. She was here to be a silent observer.

"We found your prints on the teacup and

your blood on the weapon that killed Cynthia Ellicott."

Captain Cahill sighed and rotated to face Chris head on. "I didn't realize the thing had cut me until later."

"And the teacup? Seems pretty sloppy."

The captain shrugged. "Someone would have noticed if I was wearing gloves."

"That's why you went back and touched the cup after Aunt Agatha died." Kalina couldn't help herself.

Both Chris and the captain looked at her. "I saw it in a picture on Facebook."

"I guess I should have been more careful."

"You had to know you wouldn't get away with it," Chris said.

"I nearly did. You had Margaret Grant in for questioning. If you hadn't noticed that damn little speck of blood you would have charged her with at least one murder. Probably both."

"Would it have been worth it?"

Captain Cahill let out a bitter bark of laughter.

"They killed my father. They lied and put him in jail. He couldn't handle it in there and so he took the easy way out." His eyes shone with unshed tears. "My mother thought by moving away we could escape the shame but it never left me. Oh, I wasn't ashamed of my father. I knew he hadn't hurt that girl. But the injustice stuck with me."

Chris loosened his grip on his gun. "So you came back as a cop, hoping people wouldn't remember you."

"I left here as a child. People change a lot in thirty years. I made sure when my predecessor retired, I was in the right place at the right time to assume his position. I knew people wouldn't think I could be behind it."

"The car accident with Alan Grant. That was you too," Kalina said. She just couldn't keep her mouth shut.

"Clever aren't you? Yes, that was me too. He had my father's case forced on him. And can you believe he went on to marry one of the witnesses who put my father away? They had to pay for their crime."

"What about Adam Jenkins?" Chris posed.

Cahill shook his head. "That was a lucky coincidence."

Chris holstered his gun and pulled a pair of handcuffs from his belt. "I need you stand up."

Captain Cahill again complied without argument. He got to his feet and turned around, hands behind his back. The officers who had been on the periphery approached, weapons aimed at the ground. Chris snapped the cuffs in place. "Daniel Cahill, you are under arrest for the murders of Alan Grant, Cynthia Ellicott and Agatha Davies and the attempted murder of Margaret Grant. You have the right to remain silent. Anything you say can and will be used against you in a court of law. You have a right to an attorney to be present during questioning. If you cannot afford an attorney, one will be provided for you. Do you understand these rights as I have read them to you?"

"Yes. I am waiving my right to counsel and I would like to give a written confession."

Kalina hadn't been expecting that response.

If it shocked Chris, he didn't show it. He just led Captain Cahill through the maze of headstones and back to the car. He situated the man in the back seat before turning to address Kalina. "Thank you again. We can take it from here."

"Sure. I'm just glad I could help."

She watched both cars pull out of the parking lot and head down Main Street toward the station. She wasn't sure what to do so just started walking. With the killer caught, there wasn't much left to do but wait for the trial, if there even was one. If Captain Cahill was refusing a lawyer and willing to sign a confession, something told her a trial might not be in the cards.

15

Monday morning came as a shock to the system for Kalina. She hadn't heard anything else from Chris but she wasn't expecting to. At ten minutes to nine, she flipped the front door sign to "OPEN" and settled behind the counter, ready for an influx of teenagers and older patrons. After all, she had a host of new arrivals waiting to be distributed. She'd given AJ the day off from helping out, given everything he had gone through. He seemed grateful to just be a kid for a little while. He had plenty of time to grow up.

The stillness of the shop wrapped itself around her, seeping into her thoughts, and calmed her.

The bell sounded above the front door and jarred her out of her trance. Chris stood in the doorway, framed by morning light. He was dressed in jeans and a t-shirt. He looked exhausted. Kalina stood up and approached him.

"Hi."

"Uh, hey. I hope this isn't a bad time."

She made a show of looking around the shop. "Perfect time. How are you?"

"Honestly, I'm still trying to process everything. Dan, he wrote out a confession yesterday. He's meeting with the prosecutor to discuss a plea. Avoid trial. He's going to do time and a lot of it."

"I know you looked up to him."

"I thought he was a good guy. Good police officer. I guess I never realized just how much darkness he was carrying around with him. I can't imagine going through what he went through. And it kills me that I even feel sorry for him."

"Vigilante justice isn't right but sometimes the system is broken and making things right gets messy." She motioned to the stacks of comics. "Isn't that what most of these are about?"

"I guess you're right."

"Has there been any word on Mrs. Grant?"

"It sounds like they got her stabilized. She's going to make it but they said she's probably going to have some nerve damage from the arsenic."

"How awful."

"I was going to head over and let her know that we caught Dan. Would you like to come with me?"

"Are you sure that's appropriate?"

"If it wasn't for you, Kal, she'd probably be dead and the case would still be open. I couldn't have done this without you."

"If you can wait a few hours I'll close up for lunch and we can go over."

"Yeah, of course. I don't know why I expected you to just drop everything. You have a business to run."

"I'll see you over at the hospital at noon, okay?"

He didn't say anything, just pulled her into a tight hug. She held on tight too. She hadn't been imagining the way they were falling back into each other's orbits. Maybe there was something there to rekindle.

She let that thought buoy her through the morning. By noon she was ready to get out of the shop. She hung up the lunch sign and locked the front door. Chris waited for her just outside the shop. The hospital was at the other end of town from the waterfront. It afforded easier access in case of accidents on the highway. They checked in at the front desk and were escorted to the ICU. Mrs. Grant lay in bed, her skin ashen and her eyes half-closed. But she was most definitely alive.

"Mrs. Grant? It's Kalina. I wanted to see how you were doing," Kalina said and took a seat at the woman's bedside.

Mrs. Grant roused herself and turned to face her. "You told him, didn't you?"

"I had to. But we know you didn't do anything to Cynthia or Agatha. We caught the person responsible. He's going to jail for a very long time."

"Who?" She coughed. "Who was it?"

"Daniel Cahill. He was Samuel Gordon's son."

Silent tears streamed down Mrs. Grant's sunken cheeks. "I should have known." She looked directly at Chris. "We were going to come forward and admit what we did. We talked about it. I'm sorry I wasn't truthful with you before."

"Do you know who really killed Alice Beech?"

Mrs. Grant's eyes suddenly shown with tears. "Yes. There was a car speeding away that night and we did see his face. But it wasn't Samuel Gordon. It was the Police Captain's son, Andrew Paxton. The officers on the scene knew it , too, but I guess Sam had been pulled over for speeding that night and they just decided to make him the scapegoat. I'm assuming it was Captain Paxton's orders. Alan was good friends with him and agreed to take the case to keep Andrew out of jail." Tears trickled down her pale cheeks.

"Why did you lie?" Chris asked from the foot of the bed.

"The captain threatened us. At first, anyway. Then he tried to bribe us. In the end Alan convinced me that we were well liked enough in town to be believable. It was the biggest regret of my life."

"Did you marry him to keep the secret?"

"He'd already proposed. After a while it just sort of faded into the past."

Chris just nodded. "Good luck with your recovery, Mrs. Grant."

The admission about coming forward seemed to tire Mrs. Grant out and Kalina and Chris soon left her to rest. As they wound their way back to the front of the hospital, neither of them spoke.

"Are you going to charge her with perjury?"

"I think she's been through enough hell. She's going to be living with a permanent reminder of what she did and what it cost her. That's enough."

"That's really kind of you."

"I wouldn't call it that. But I don't see the point in putting an old woman behind bars at this point." He pulled out his phone. "I am going to have Andrew Paxton and his father arrested. Alice Beech is going to get the justice she deserved."

"I'm glad Sam's death won't have been for nothing." She checked her phone. "Hey, I'm still on lunch for another half hour. You want to come back and finish that game of Zombie Dice?"

"You're on."

They lazily made their way back to the shop, sequestered themselves in the back room with lunch and started the game over. Kalina even let him go first. As the dice clattered around the table in a bid to escape, a sense of normalcy settled over the shop and its two inhabitants. While darkness and death had touched the town, it would soon be pushed to the back of the townspeople's collective memory. Ellesworth would resume being a nice, waterfront, Massachusetts town. There was little chance Kalina would get wrapped up in another case of wrongful convictions and vigilante justice. She was just a comic book shop owner, after all.

QUICK AUTHOR'S NOTE

WHEN I STARTED THIS SERIES, I'LL ADMIT I didn't have the greatest grasp on writing cozies. MI did, however, enjoy the fact that I was creating a younger sleuth who could be spunky. y biggest mistake was not giving Kalina a real reason to investigate the case, especially as she'd been gone from town for a while. And for a long time (like 5 years) there was a version out there where she just noses her way in and solves the case. But readers left consistent feedback over time that they didn't like that she didn't have a reason and to be honest, I'd recently been thinking about that, too.

So, I went back and I edited and tweaked the story a little. The main plot hadn't changed much but I strengthened her connection to the case and I tried to up the romance angle a little more. Overall, I think it's a stronger story in this form and I hope that you all enjoyed it.

Somehow I got the personal connection memo on book 2 because Kalina has a much stronger link to the case from the start. I thought it would be interesting to explore how people we thought we once knew could change and be capable of horrific things.

TURN THE PAGE TO GET A GLIMPSE AT *FORGIVE and Forget...*

<u>FORGIVE AND FORGET</u>

Murder hits close to home.

When her childhood best friend is implicated in her own father's murder, Kalina can't help nosing in and uses her newly rekindled relationship with the town's top detective to find the truth.

· · ·

As the facts stack up against her friend, Kalina is left to wonder: is she guilty of patricide or are her fractured memories the result of a more sinister, years' long mind game?

Read on for a sneak peek of *Forgive and Forget...*

An unusually oppressive early morning summer heat shimmered on the pavement as Kalina Greystone took off at a steady jog from the front of her shop, Geeks and Things. She had barely taken enough steps to get to the next block on Main Street when her phone beeped at her, displaying the temperature: 81 degrees. At seven in the morning.

"Wonderful," she groaned before settling on a playlist and picking up the pace. Heat or no heat, she needed to get her run in before she had to open up for the day.

The end of summer was a big money maker for the shop, especially with kids getting ready for school. There was little doubt in her mind that most of the teenagers in town would be turning in summer reading lists crammed with comics and graphic novels. She only felt a little guilty that the next generation wasn't reading actual books.

The notion that this was *her* shop, *her* livelihood, had finally settled in. People in town had stopped comparing the way she ran the business to her father—at least to her face—and it made the decision to come back home to Ellesworth feel like the right call. The little seaside town moved at a slower pace to the city, where she'd spent most of her adult life, but it had some perks, too. She'd managed to reconnect and rekindle a spark with her high school sweetheart, Christian Harper.

Kalina took a sharp left and sucked in a deep breath as she took the hill leading in the direction of the cemetery and the town's one church. As her heart pounded in her ears from the exertion, she flashed back to three months ago when she and Chris had stood in the cemetery and solved a pair of murders. The frenzy surrounding Aunt Agatha and Ms. Ellicott's passing had finally died down and the town was back to being quaint and normal. Kalina's phone buzzed in her pocket and she pulled it out to see a text from Chris asking her if they were still on for dinner. She smiled and slowed to a walk before responding that they were definitely on for dinner. They were lucky that their first break-up had been amicable. They were on different life tracks and they had been mature enough to get that. When he held her hand or kissed her goodnight she still felt like a giddy schoolgirl. Of course, she'd dated in college and grad school but being with Chris now was different. They were finally in a place where they could be together as adults and make it work.

Phone stowed back in her pocket, Kalina took off at a sprint to make it up and over the hill and settle back into a comfortable pace. As she ran she spotted Theo Maxwell in his boxers and undershirt scooping up the morning paper. He blushed bright red and waved before darting back inside. She chuckled to herself and took the next right, heading past the church. The door eased open and a lone figure stepped out looking subdued and tired. Leslie Mayfair, the former almost-Mrs. Cahill. A pang of sadness tightened Kalina's chest as she watched the usually bubbly school teacher hunch her shoulders on her way to her car. She hadn't known her fiancé had been killing little old ladies for sending his innocent father to prison. They made eye contact for a brief, uncomfortable moment and Kalina opened her mouth to say 'Good morning' but held her tongue. Leslie yanked her car door open and climbed into the driver seat.

Kalina waited until the car was out of sight before continuing her morning circuit. Sweat glistened on her bare arms and matted her short, auburn curls to her forehead as she veered away from the church and out towards the coast. Only a handful of people lived out by the water these days thanks to beach erosion. The salty air was a few degrees cooler and she sucked in a big gulp. Trying to shake the unease from seeing Leslie, Kalina put on another burst of speed and took the rolling slope of Ocean Front Lane at a decent clip. Her phone vibrated again and, in her earbuds, an automated voice announced that AJ was calling.

"Answer call," she said and slowed to a walk. "Hey, AJ, what are you doing up this early?"

"Hey, Aunt K. I was just checking in. I wanted to see if you needed help at the store today," her nephew answered.

He had done a lot of 'checking in' in the last couple months. Not that she minded. It put her mind at ease that he was doing okay after watching Aunt Agatha die. "If you want to stop by this afternoon you can. I don't know that I'll have too much for you to do, though."

"Great. Are you okay?"

Kalina continued along Ocean Front at a slow pace, getting her heart rate back down to normal. "Yeah, I'm just out for a run."

"Oh. You've been doing that a lot since…"

He didn't have to finish the thought for her know what he meant. "We all cope in different ways. And I could use the exercise."

Kalina rounded a bend in the street and a three-story house came into view. It belonged to the Larrabees. She'd been friends with their daughter, Nadine, in high school. Normally it wouldn't have drawn her attention in the cookie-cutter section of town. Today, she stopped and stood with her mouth hanging open. A man's body lay prone in the middle of the house's small driveway and a woman about Kalina's age sat on the front steps, rocking back and forth.

"Aunt K., are you there?" AJ's voice sounded tinny in her earbuds.

"I have to call you back," she said and yanked the buds from her ears. She moved into view slowly so as not to startle the woman. "Nadine?"

The woman looked up and Kalina saw her eyes shine with fresh tears. At this distance she could see Nadine's hands covered in what Kalina assumed was blood. A dark stain had spread under the man's head on the asphalt. "Oh, God. What did I do?" Nadine whimpered.

Kalina pulled the cord out of the head-phone jack of her phone and dialed 911. She waited for the operator to give the standard response before speaking. "I need an ambulance at 1609 Ocean Front Lane. Send the police, too. A man is dead."

Forgive and Forget *is available on all storefronts - find it on your favorite store today!*

A FREE STORY
FOR YOU...

Enjoyed *Pains and Penalties* but don't want the mystery to end? You can sign up for my newsletter by clicking here and receive *Toil and Trouble*, a fun Halloween romp with Kalina, right away as my thank you for signing up and choosing to hang out with me.

Subscribe and find out now!

ABOUT THE AUTHOR

S.E. Biglow is the pen name of *USA Today* best-selling author Sarah Biglow. She lives in Massachusetts with her husband and son. She is a licensed attorney and spends her days combatting employment discrimination as an Investigator with the Massachusetts Commission Against Discrimination.

You can find an up-to-date list of all my books here